SUSPICION

JAMES LALONDE
BOOK 1

A. D. HAY

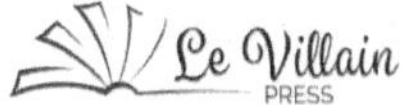
Le Villain
PRESS

Suspicion. A James Lalonde Mystery Novella, Book 1
Copyright © A. D. Hay (2020, 2022). All rights reserved.

Third Edition. Previously Published as MISSING

www.authoradhay.com

ISBN-13: 978-1-9163483-2-5 (paperback)

Book cover design by Le Villain Book Covers at levillainbookcovers.com

FRENCH IN SUSPICION

Conservateur: *noun.* Curator, custodian, or keeper.

Merde: *noun.* A mild, humorous substitute for "shit."

Papi: *noun.* Grandpa, Grandfather

ONE

SUNDAY: 11:38 P.M.

ELIZABETH STAGGERED through the front door and let it swing shut behind her. A sharp pain shot through her head as the loud bang broke the silence in the apartment. Her long, thin fingers brushed against the smooth wall to her left, but nothing was there.

Wrong way, stupid.

She patted the wall, then realised light would only make things worse. Not only would it add a new level of intensity to her headache, but the light would also highlight the thin layer of dust along the skirting boards, the dirty dishes in the kitchen sink, and the clothes lying over the turquoise ottoman at the end of her bed. These were all things she had promised to take care of last weekend, and the clutter was visible the second she opened the front door.

Admitting defeat, she turned around and toggled the deadbolt latch. Her heels clacked against the wooden floorboards as she walked down the dark hall of her apartment, just as she had every evening. The blackout curtains she had purchased a few days earlier were having the desired effect. If only they would help her sleep. As she inched up the hallway toward her bedroom, Elizabeth ran her fingers along the wall.

She paused, and the walls spun around her. She was drunker than she'd thought. Now she was lightheaded, disoriented, and in the dark. Her financial troubles and any plans of late-night research were on hold. She needed to sleep this off.

Earlier that evening, she'd had dinner with the curators of the British Museum. The evening was a complete disaster. These dinners were about networking and securing funds for the next phase of the archaeological dig at Tintagel, but all she had achieved was no funds, more research, and a headache.

Nine months had passed since she'd returned from Cornwall. Sifting through soil and finding fragments of a bygone world was her favourite part of the job. Not that she didn't love research, but it was often challenging. Money always ran out during the research-and-analysis phase of a dig, meaning that she had to raise more funds. This fundraising took time away from research, creating a vicious cycle.

She was fortunate that the Northampton Museum of Anthropology had funded the initial stage of the dig, but the museum was niche and small, not a bottomless pit of cash. The museum had a small number of investors and received government funding on the side. With this allocation of funds came the requirement to justify how the recipient's time and money were spent. That was the thing about investors. They all had the same goals: a high return, low risk, and quick results. It was up to her to find another way to raise funds and to continue the research. But she couldn't do anything tonight.

Leaning against the wall for support, she inched closer to her open bedroom door, stumbled through the doorway, and threw herself onto her bed. As she gazed up at the white space above, her hairpins poked into her scalp. Elizabeth shook off her red patent heels and pulled at her hair. A slight smile formed on her ruby lips as the sharp digging sensation subsided.

She thought about changing into something more comfortable, but any attempt to unzip her dress would only cause her to become dizzier. The room had stopped spinning and she wasn't prepared to upset that delicate equilibrium. Her straightened, but normally curly, black hair fell across her golden-brown skin as she continued to pull the pins out. As she fixed her dark-brown eyes straight ahead, her heavy eyelids closed.

———

PRESSED up against the wall of the dining room, Pippa Baker hung back in the shadows, clutching a black bag and waiting for Elizabeth to go about her night-time routine. She heard movement coming from somewhere within the apartment and, in an attempt to decipher the location of the sound, turned her ear towards the wall between the dining room and the hallway.

Elizabeth must be home.

Pippa was petite and had long brown hair. She had moved from Cambridge, Massachusetts, to Northampton to start a master's degree programme and gain experience in archaeology. She had met Elizabeth on the first day of her internship.

After a few moments, Pippa walked across the hallway to Elizabeth's home office. Elizabeth had a habit of taking her work home with her. This habit made Pippa's next task all too easy. Pippa navigated around Elizabeth's desk at the centre of the room and paused to admire the three framed paintings of the French chateaux at Pierrefonds, Comtal, and Chantilly.

Journals, textbooks, and several PhD theses—all marked

with sticky notes—stood in tall piles across the archaeologist's white-stained oak desk. A white bookcase spanned the right-hand side of the room, creating an L shape towards the door. Rows of books, all on just two topics—anthropology and archaeology—lined the shelves.

Enclosed in a long glass box on the bookshelf was a Celtic sword. Pippa walked to the bookshelf and placed her black bag on the floor. Brushing her hair over her shoulder, she lifted the lid of the glass box and pulled out the sword, careful not to cut herself on its broken blade. The long, thin handle glistened in the moonlight that shone from between the thick curtains as Pippa stared at the old Cornish inscription. She knelt down, picked up her black bag, and pulled out a long piece of white linen. After neatly wrapping the Celtic sword, she placed it inside the bag.

Pippa knew it was a bad career move to steal an artefact and sell it to a private buyer. In the archaeological world, it earned the culprit a certain reputation. If caught, she would need to find a new profession. As a teenager, she had dreamed of becoming an archaeologist and excavating in the beautiful deserts of Egypt. But that was all just a fantasy. A childish fantasy. The reality of modern archaeology was so different from the image she'd created in her mind.

As she closed the glass case, she heard furniture scraping against the wall. Pippa froze.

Shit, she must be awake.

Her eyes widened, and her heart raced as she listened to the movements, hoping Elizabeth wouldn't come into her office. But it was useless to panic. There was only one logical thing to do.

Pippa tiptoed up the hall towards the main bedroom. She paused and looked over her shoulder. Tiny hairs on the back of her neck stood on end. No one was there. She wasn't superstitious or easily spooked, but she could have sworn someone was watching her. She knew it. Perhaps the adrenaline rush of the break-in had heightened Pippa's senses and caused her to become paranoid. Besides, it wasn't a break-in if someone had the key, she'd reassured herself as she planned every detail of this operation.

Pippa refocused her attention towards the open bedroom door at the end of the hall.

What is she doing?

As she reached the bedroom, she saw the source of the loud snoring. It was coming from the next room, the living room. The light from the moon pierced through the tiny crack between the thick, heavy curtains, highlighting Elizabeth. She was lying on the sofa with her mouth wide open and a pair of red heels lay scattered across the room. She was still in the same black dress she'd left the museum in over ten hours ago.

Pippa lifted an eyebrow and cocked her head to the side as she clutched the bag close to her chest. On the couch, Elizabeth was stirring. Pippa held her breath as she watched Elizabeth wheeze and gurgle then roll onto her side. She needed to get out of there before Elizabeth woke up. She looked down at the sleeping archaeologist then stepped into the shadows, away from the light.

As she plotted her exit, Pippa once again felt that she wasn't alone. It was as if she had an audience watching her every move. She froze. She turned around, half expecting to see someone standing in the doorway between the hall and the living room. No one was there.

Don't panic.

That was the last thing she needed to do. With heightened senses and anxiety came mistakes. Right now, she had to focus. Pippa needed to get out of there before Elizabeth woke up.

Pippa gasped as she felt the coolness of a sharp blade thrust into her back. She looked to her left. In the reflection of the darkened television screen was the outline of a dark figure standing behind her. So, she wasn't paranoid.

Pippa dropped the black bag and pressed her hand against

her chest, struggling to breathe. As she fought for air, she felt a sharp pain as the knife was pulled out and her lungs filled with blood. The room spun, and the carpet of Elizabeth's living room drew nearer by the second. What hurt most was the betrayal. Worst of all, she hadn't seen it coming until it was too late.

TWO

JAMES LALONDE DROPPED his keys into the small bowl on top of the dark wooden shoe cabinet next to the front door. A little chirp cried out from the smartphone in his pocket. More work, the perfect way to spend the last twenty-two minutes of his Sunday evening.

Valentine is going to scream at me.

That was how every Sunday evening played out. He expected this weekend to be no different. Piles of editing and an angry girlfriend screaming at him in French.

As chief editor of the *Northampton Tribune*, James had a mountain of work to climb and would never reach its summit. He sighed. This was not the job he had wished for as a fresh-faced student. He had dreamed of investigative journalism and the same clichéd fantasies every journalism student imagined: writing in war zones, uncovering government secrets, and exposing corruption. And maybe one day, when he was too old to chase down stories, he would become the chief editor of a newspaper. He'd received his wish, but it had come thirty years too early. And now he longed for the adrenaline rush that came with chasing a story.

James walked down the hall and dumped his bag on the chair at the end of the kitchen table. He pulled out his phone and stared at the screen—he needed to assess the damage. Two messages had come through. The first was his best friend Liam wanting to catch up, and then there was the second. As usual, Harry Lancaster, the owner of the Northampton Tribune, wanted to Skype about the layout of page one. On James's first day as editor, Harry had promised to guide him through his new role. After a year, Harry would step back and observe the paper from afar. Three years later, and this was the man's idea of stepping back. But James had expected that. Harry had the reputation of being hands-on and epitomised the Oxford dictionary's definition of micromanagement.

He sighed as he continued to stare at his screen. Out of the corner of his eye, he noticed a handwritten envelope with his name on it on the kitchen table.

A large stone formed in the pit of his stomach as he recognised the handwriting. He looked around the room and listened to the silence of the house.

'Valentine,' he called out into the emptiness, but he got no response.

Silence was never a good sign, especially from Valentine. He had expected her to lecture him about his work addiction the second he stepped through the front door. But this evening was different. He was all alone.

He took a deep breath, reached out, and slid the envelope towards him. He stared at the ink on it. A chirp cried out from his phone and disrupted the silence. He rolled his eyes. Another message had come through with one more item to add to his never-ending to-do list.

The handwriting was perfect and neat. It was as if Valentine had taken her time and not written it in a last-minute rush. She loved writing letters and had attended many calligraphy courses throughout their relationship.

This letter seemed different, though perhaps it was his overactive imagination. There was only one way to find out.

James opened the envelope, careful not to tear the letter within. Inside was a single ivory page with Valentine's message.

THREE

AS HE READ the elegant script, the faint smell of Valentine's perfume—a remnant of where her wrist had brushed the paper—took James's mind to a cold winter's afternoon three years earlier. It was January. The sun had already set, and a chilly wind howled through the platform as James wrapped his arms around Valentine's waist and drew her closer. Her eyes reminded him of new, green shoots on the first day of spring. There was something slightly hypnotic about them.

'I hate this train station. Too many bad memories,' he said with a smile as he bent to kiss her ruby-red lips.

Valentine twisted her knotted blonde hair around her neck and down her right shoulder. 'It's saying goodbye every week for the last three months that makes this hard.'

'I know.'

She reached up and kissed him on the cheek.

'Maybe I could talk to my editor and get you a position at the paper. He's always up to his eyeballs in work, and I'm sure he'd find you something. It might be a junior position, but you could move in with me so expenses would be low. That way, we wouldn't have to spend our Sunday evenings in this horrible station.'

James took a deep breath and pulled Valentine a little closer.

Her cheeks flushed dark crimson as she bit the inside of her lip and stared at the ground. 'So, you're springing this on me now, on the platform, one minute before my train leaves for London?' She looked up into his sparkling blue-green eyes.

'Hey, you hate working at the Standard.'

'James—'

'I realise the timing isn't brilliant. But I was meaning to ask you all weekend. Actually, I planned to ask you on Friday night, but I was worried you would say no.'

'So that was the reason for the romantic dinner.'

'Maybe. But every time I tried to raise the subject, you reminded me I'm not allowed to talk about work at the weekends.'

'But in answer to your question, yes, I'd love to work at your paper.' Valentine moved her hand up James's chest and around his neck, leaned in, and kissed him. 'I've got to go.'

She slipped into the carriage as the doors closed and the train rolled out of the station.

———

JAMES STARED OUT THE WINDOW, the ivory piece of paper drifting towards the floorboards. A tear trickled down his cheek. He gasped as a lone thought swirled around in his mind, jolting him back to reality. As he turned and sprinted up the stairs towards the main bedroom, James slammed the vibrating phone onto the polished tabletop. Another message had come through.

The door handle banged against the wall as James burst into the bedroom. He dived straight for the small, round, black knobs on Valentine's side of the closet. He thrust the doors open and stared at the empty void before him. A space once overflowing with clothes was now bare. His trembling hands slammed the doors shut. He turned around and walked towards the chest of drawers and opened the top ones.

They were empty.

As he closed them one by one, his eye caught the framed picture resting on top of the dresser. He grabbed it with one hand as his legs gave way and he collapsed onto the bed. Tears streamed down his cheeks, falling onto the picture of him and Valentine taken on the steps of the Northampton Museum of Anthropology, a memento from their first year together. James caught the reflection of his reddened eyes in the glass, threw the picture aside and, ran down the stairs towards the kitchen.

He picked up his phone, swiped his finger across the screen, selected her number from his contacts lists then listened to the dialling tone. 'The number you have called is not available. Please try again later,' a robotic voice called out of the handset.

'She's left me,' he whispered.

James stabbed the red button to end the call. He sighed as a Skype video call rang through to his phone. *Merde, it's Harry. I have to answer this.*

FOUR

MONDAY: 7:08 A.M.

JAMES TOOK a deep breath as he walked across the newsroom floor and darted in and out of the sea of cubicles, all lined with books, stacks of newspapers, and random printouts. Then he saw it. A sharp pain shot deep into his chest below his sternum as the empty workstation came into view. His breathing quickened as he approached the lone chair tucked into a desk. The only items that remained on the table were a computer, a monitor, a mini desk calendar, a small grey sharpener, and a phone. A grey name plaque reading "Valentine Charlet" hung on the light-grey-carpeted partition wall.

She's gone.

James surveyed the empty newsroom. Thankfully, no one was present to witness the second shattering of his heart. He had expected her not to be at work, but a naïve part of him was hoping for a second chance and thought he might catch her cleaning out her desk.

A cold hand rested on James's shoulder, breaking his concentration. James whirled around to see his senior journalist, Gavin Whitehead, standing behind him.

'If you need to talk, you know where to find me.' Gavin continued to pat James's shoulder.

'I'm fine.' James's eyes lingered on the empty cubicle.

'I can tell she left you.'

'Did Valentine say something to you?' James refocused on Gavin.

'No, she would never do that.' Gavin gave him a weak smile. 'You, however, look like shit. It's as if you've been up all night with something on your mind. Something other than work.'

James tried to hold back the tears as he stared at her empty desk. 'Great, everyone will know.'

'I'm sorry, but the best thing you can do is come up with a reason for her absence that takes the focus off your break-up,' he said as James sighed. 'There'll be fewer questions that way.'

James turned around and continued to walk toward his office. He had to reassign a story to an overloaded staff of journalists. This was never a popular decision, but it had to be done. On top of this, he had to rehire for the vacant junior position. Deep down, James knew Valentine was never coming back. She had made up her mind, and he was left to clean up the mess. James couldn't drag his feet on the rehire—he was already short-staffed.

———

THE EARLY MORNING sun shone through the window of James's office and highlighted the array of dust particles on the dark wooden tabletop. James sat on the edge of his desk and clicked the end of his pen. A group of journalists stood around watching his blue-green eyes drift up and down the notepad in his hands. His task was harder than he had imagined, especially since Valentine had arranged an interview that was due to start in less than twenty-two minutes. It was the fourth piece of bad news that he'd received in the last eight hours, but this news was courtesy of the *Tribune's* internal calendar system.

A part of his job as chief editor of the daily *Northampton Tribune* was to manage the story assignments among his team of journalists, ensure accurate fact checking, and edit every story that crossed his desk. He also had to reassign Valentine's story to an unlucky, overworked soul. Reassigning a piece was never a popular decision. But he had chosen a victim and another as a backup.

'Margaret, remind me again what you're working on.'

James continued to stare at his notepad and clenched his jaw, awaiting the inevitable response.

'I'm covering the Northampton Festival of Food and Wine,' she said. 'It's a week-long festival. And I'm doing it all on my own.'

James bit the inside of his lip and continued to stare at the list of stories.

Imagine how shitty Margaret would be if she had to edit her copy.

James glanced up at her and smiled, then refocused on the lone story on the pad with no name next to it. It was to his great pleasure that Margaret Winters had the ultimate job security. She was the sister-in-law of the owner, Harry Lancaster. James had sworn to Gavin that she spent her downtime thinking of creative ways to test his patience, and all he could do was smile and pray that Margaret would trade in her journalistic dreams for something else. But three years later, he was still praying.

'Simon, do you have time to interview—' holding the notepad and pen in one hand, James looked down at the phone on his desk, tapped the home button, and read the notes on the screen, '—Elizabeth Carmichael about the Arthurian Exhibit in the Northampton Museum of Anthropology?'

'I'm sorry, but I have three film reviews to write, one of

which is exclusive to the online edition. And I need to see two of those films.' Simon forced a smile.

'Yes.' James stared at the notes on the screen. 'I don't recall seeing that review on my desk.'

James looked up at Simon and raised his eyebrows.

Simon rubbed the back of his neck and looked at the floor, avoiding James's gaze. 'Yeah, I'm a little behind.'

James returned his gaze to the pad in his hand and scraped the end of his pen through his thick, dark-blond hair and along his scalp. He rolled his eyes. If he continued to go through his journalists in this manner, he would end up with the same result—an unassigned story and white space in the paper's culture section.

Part of him wanted to leap at the chance of stepping out of the editor's chair and pursuing a story, even if it was an interview with a curator of a small museum. He was desperate for a change of scenery, and this surprised him.

How long is it going to take to interview someone about a small exhibit?

James threw the notepad on his desk.

FIVE

MONDAY: 8:40 A.M.

A PAIR of thick wooden doors towered above him. James pressed the buzzer once more, then stood back and waited. A few moments later, he used the drop handle to knock on the door. He checked his watch. It was twenty minutes to nine, and she was late.

Merde.

Two minutes later, a shuffling sound was followed by a groan as the double doors moved towards him. He stepped back, and a short woman in her late fifties, her ash-blonde hair cut in a shoulder-length bob, peered out from behind the door.

'The museum doesn't open until nine,' the woman grumbled as she narrowed her eyes at James.

'One of my journalists, Valentine Charlet, had an appointment with Elizabeth Carmichael. It was due to start ten minutes ago.' James forced a smile. 'She returned to Paris, and I'm conducting the interview in her place.'

'I don't have time for this,' the woman said as her voice quaked.

Please don't cry.

The woman's eyes filled up, and a single tear ran down her cheek.

'Let's call Elizabeth on her phone, and I'll be on my way.'

The woman sighed as she leaned against the door. 'Sorry, I'm having a bad day. That's all.' She turned around and walked past the ticket booths, towards the spiral staircase. 'You're not the only one to inquire about her today.'

'Are you Elizabeth's boss?' James was a little out of breath as he attempted to keep up with her.

'Oh, sorry, no. I'm Catherine Gallagher. I'm the receptionist.'

As he reached the top of the staircase and walked through the second set of doors, James surveyed the numerous anthropological artefacts sleeping in their glass cases. Catherine darted towards the stairs to their left and ascended to the upper mezzanine level.

'The administration section is up here,' Catherine said over her shoulder as she continued to scale the stairs.

James dashed up the steps and followed Catherine towards a large birch door bearing the label "Administration." A deafening bang filled the sleepy museum as the door bounced off the wall, and Catherine disappeared out of his line of sight.

James followed her into the administration offices and propped against the reception desk as he listened to her call. She slammed the phone down.

'She's not answering.' Catherine ran her fingers through her hair and hit the redial button on the switchboard.

'Maybe she's just running late.'

Catherine shook her head. 'You don't understand. Elizabeth is a workaholic. She's always the first to arrive and often kicked out by Security at the end of every night. This is not normal behaviour for her. She has a fantastic memory. It's not like her to forget.'

I need this interview.

'If she's as bad as you're letting on, then she's most likely at home, working. Maybe her phone is flat or on silent, and she's lost track of time.'

Catherine hesitated and looked at James as she listened to the dial tone. 'Maybe that's plausible,' she muttered a few moments later.

'I could stop by her house to see if she's okay and report back to you, but I'll need her address.'

'I can't give out that information.'

'You're worried about Elizabeth, and I'm risking white space in my culture section if I don't get this interview. The interview is about the new exhibit that's opening soon. This is in the museum's best interest,' James said. 'And besides, if I find out what's happened to her, it will be one less thing for you to worry about.'

Catherine hunched over her computer and stared at the screen. James straightened and tapped his fingers on the reception desk. He could see Harry's look of disgust at the white space in the culture section. It was possible to move things around, but getting this interview was the easiest way of avoiding the drama.

'You didn't get this from me.' Catherine handed him a business card with a handwritten address on the back.

James read the inscription and nodded to Catherine. 'I'll call you.'

It wasn't the first time he had said that to a middle-aged woman.

SIX

MONDAY: 7:55 A.M.

ELIZABETH OPENED her eyes as the bright morning sun shone through the curtains. She squeezed her eyes shut. The light was too bright, and it was far too early. A sharp pain shot through her skull. That was the price for last night's drinking. She opened her eyes again and blinked as the room came into view. Elizabeth gripped her forehead as she recognised her surroundings.

I don't remember falling asleep here.

Elizabeth threw her legs off the couch and dragged her weary body to her feet. As she shuffled through the living room, she stepped into a pool of liquid. It ran through her toes and seeped into her pantyhose. As she staggered across the living room, Elizabeth tripped over a heavy object. Reaching out, she steadied herself with the aid of her entertainment unit. She looked down to find her assistant, Pippa Baker, lying face down in a pool of what she could only assume was Pippa's blood.

Her body clenched as a rock formed in the pit of her stomach.

What happened last night?

She looked at her bloodstained pantyhose and tried to

recall the events from the previous night, which was a blur. She remembered struggling to open the door of the taxi and staggering inside, but after that, everything was a little hazy. Her memory had large gaps.

Who would do this to Pippa? What was she doing here?

Elizabeth stared at Pippa's body, then she remembered. She whirled around and sprinted down the short hallway, then took a right turn into her office. It was just as she had expected.

A glass case was resting on her white bookshelves, just as it had every day since she'd moved it into her home. But this time, it was empty.

My career is over.

The artefact was never supposed to leave the museum, but she was addicted to her work and broke the rules and brought it home for research. Now, she would pay the price. As she contemplated the repercussions of the events that had unfolded in her house, she lifted her shaking hand and covered her mouth.

Then another realisation struck her, this one far worse than the first.

I have no memory of, or alibi for, anything that unfolded after dinner.

She gasped as she recalled a moment from earlier that day.

Could I have done this? What did I do with the sword? Did I take it to London?

Tears streamed down her face as she hobbled towards her desk and sat down. For the second time in three years, life as she knew it was over. Through her sea of tears, Elizabeth saw a small, beige tag lying on the floor with a catalogue number written on it. She reached over, picked it up, and slipped it into her pocket.

Elizabeth trekked back to the living room. It was time to call the police. The longer she waited, the more suspicious she would appear, and that was the last thing she needed on top of her workload.

With a sigh, Elizabeth gazed at Pippa's lifeless body. *Why can't I remember anything? I need to stop drinking like this.* Then she realised there was a call that she needed to make first. Scrolling through her contacts, Elizabeth winced as a name flashed across the screen. She had to tell him. Striking the screen with her index finger, Elizabeth listened to the dial tone as she braced herself for the inevitable fallout.

'Hello,' a refined English accent said on the other end of the line.

'It's happened, again.'

'What did you do this time?'

Elizabeth's posture stiffened. 'I, I—'

'If you don't tell me, I can't help you.'

'Pippa is dead,' Elizabeth sobbed.

'What?'

'I found her on my living room floor when I woke up. I can't remember how I got home. But I made a call to Pippa last night.' Elizabeth continued to sob.

'Yesterday, you were at her throat. I thought you were going to leap across the table and strangle her. And you have been known to get violent when you're drunk.'

Her chest tightened. 'I have a DUI, and then there's the domestic violence report,' Elizabeth said as she let out a strangled sob. 'I'm screwed.'

'Nonsense, I'll get you a good lawyer. And I won't tell the police that you confessed. I'll think of another reason you called. Let me think for a moment.'

'There's one more thing.'

'It better not be another body.'

'It's missing. I took it home from work.'

'Oh, shit.'

Elizabeth's hands trembled. 'I'm going to be the first

person the police suspect. They'll take one look at my record; I'll be under suspicion after that.'

'What about the murder weapon?'

She peered down at Pippa's body. 'It's not here. I think she's been stabbed.'

'Touch nothing. Call the police, but don't mention the arguments you've been having. Just mention that you're shocked that she was even in your apartment.'

As Elizabeth opened her mouth, a dial tone screeched from her phone. *Where's the murder weapon?* Turning around, she dashed down the hall. As she reached the front door, she glanced to her right. Sitting in the middle of the kitchen bench was a knife block set with a missing knife. *I'm screwed.*

SEVEN

MONDAY: 9:55 A.M.

A MELODIC PING chimed as the doors of the elevator sprang open on the third floor of the apartment building. James read the directions and followed the corridor around to Elizabeth's apartment. A crowd of people were lined up against the wall, peering down the hall towards a partially opened door.

Oh, merde.

James looked at his phone and clicked the home button, then read the email on the screen. A thick yellow tape stretched across the width of the hallway in front of him. He leaned forward and squinted as he tried to read the number on the door down the hall. It was no use—he couldn't read the shiny silver number at this distance.

Maybe it's just a break-in?

Just what he needed. Getting this interview was not as easy as he'd first thought. His inner chief editor could see the blank space in the culture section of tomorrow's paper. But worst-case scenario, he could push the piece back until Friday, the first day of the Arthurian Exhibit at the Northampton Museum of Anthropology. So, he had until Thursday to interview Elizabeth, write and edit his story, and complete a long list of other tasks.

No more panicking.

James stood aside as a photographer and a police officer lifted the tape and walked down the hall.

'Officer.' James pushed his way through the small crowd.

A short man of Malaysian descent turned around and walked towards him.

'Sorry, no press allowed,' he said as James looked down and read his badge.

'Constable Chan, I have an interview with Elizabeth Carmichael. One of my journalists, Valentine Charlet, had an appointment at nine, but she moved back to Paris. I'm covering her story. Do you know where I can find Elizabeth?' James grabbed the police tape and lifted it up.

'So, you have an interview. You realise I've heard that one before.' PC David Chan positioned himself in front of the tape and blocked James's entry into the crime scene.

James inched forward and pulled his smartphone out of his pocket.

'Your name?' Chan asked as he gripped the two-way on his shoulder.

'James Lalonde, the *Northampton Tribune*,' James said as Chan released his grip on the radio.

'This is a crime scene. I can't let you in.'

'I'm not here for your crime scene. I'm here because this is the location of my interview. Why can't you tell me where I can find the woman I'm supposed to meet? If you don't give me answers, I will go over your head.'

'Fine, you do that, then.' Chan continued to stand at the yellow tape in front of James.

'Look, I know you're just doing your job—'

'Oh, so you don't have connections,' Chan said. 'You're not the first journalist to come here this morning with this same story, but the other guy wasn't as persistent as you.'

'Why can't you just tell me what's really going on here?'

'This is a crime scene. It's on a need-to-know basis. And you don't need to know,' Chan said, still clutching the yellow tape.

'If you tell me where I can find Elizabeth Carmichael, I'll be out of here.' James pointed towards the lift. 'Or maybe I should leave and talk to DCI Anwar Khan about my experiences with you?'

Chan stood tall and unchanged. Usually, the sheer murmur of that man's name got James what he wanted, but not this time.

'Go right ahead.' Chan crossed his arms and pursed his lips as he stared at James. 'He's running the investigation from behind the scenes at the office. I trust you know where that is.'

James sprinted towards the elevator.

———

JAMES STRUCK the bottom of Detective Chief Inspector Anwar Khan's door with the toe of his brown boot. The searing heat from the double espressos seeped through the paper cups and burned the tips of his fingers. A murmur came from behind a large pile of folders bearing the Northamptonshire police logo.

'Coffee?' a voice questioned from the back of the office.

'Anwar?' James tried not to laugh.

Anwar's head popped up from behind the mountains of paperwork, his dark brown eyes wide with surprise. 'What have you done now?'

'I'm a little offended, but I'll let that one slide,' James said with a smirk.

Anwar stood, then ambled around his desk towards James. 'You leave a trail of trouble in your wake. Why would this time be any different?'

'Ouch.' James handed Anwar one of the double espressos.

'So, this is what a promotion looks like at the Northamptonshire Police,' he said with a bemused smile.

'I guess this should look familiar to you.' Anwar lifted the lid off the espresso and took a sip. 'Are you sure you're not Italian? You're obsessed with coffee.'

James took a deep breath, then smiled as he took a sip of his own espresso. It was now or never.

'I met PC Chan at Elizabeth Carmichael's apartment, and he refused to tell me any details concerning her whereabouts.'

'I knew you were here for a reason.' Anwar pushed a hand through his thick hair in frustration, as he turned and trekked back to his desk.

'You're not the only one here with a job to do.'

'Yes, but I'm not looking for a front-page story,' Anwar snapped.

'Actually, Valentine had an interview with her about a new exhibit at the anthropology museum. She couldn't make it, so I'm conducting the interview for her.'

'One of the many perks of sleeping with the chief editor.'

'All I need to know is where she is so I can be on my way to conduct my interview.' James waved his hand around and struck the door. 'Then I'll be out of your hair. That's clearly what you want.'

Anwar stared at his desk, his bushy eyebrows knotted in concentration. He sipped the espresso while jotting notes in a spiral-bound, pocket-sized notebook. The sea of paperwork had grown since James was last in Anwar's office, but that wasn't the only thing that had changed. His office smelled like a closed-down paper mill. The once ordered and tidy office was now a tip. Anwar scribbled a series of scrawled notes. As he turned the page, James caught a serial number with a short note—NMA-642901A, Tag found in her pocket.

A few moments later, Anwar looked up from his desk and shook his head. 'What are you expecting me to tell you? It's an ongoing investigation.'

Now I'm interested. Very interested.

'My story is for the culture section.' James walked over to the edge of Anwar's desk and put down his half-empty espresso cup. 'All I want is to find Elizabeth and talk to her.' James straightened and placed his hands on his hips.

'James, I—'

James laughed. 'You have her in custody. I'm not leaving until you let me speak with her.'

'Yes, she's in police custody.' The detective stood up and stared at James. 'At seven fifty-five a.m. this morning, Elizabeth Carmichael awoke to find her assistant, Pippa Baker, lying face down in a pool of her own blood.' Anwar held up his finger as James opened his mouth. 'We have a train ticket that gives her enough time to arrive home and be present for the murder.'

Anwar walked around the room and closed the door behind them. As James turned around, he noticed a business card from Dr Olivier Deschamps, a local pathologist, laying on Anwar's desk.

'You won't know this for sure until you receive the autopsy results.'

'What I'm about to tell you is off the record.'

James nodded as he picked the espresso cup off the desk.

'James.' Anwar glared at him.

'I get it.' James took a sip of his espresso. 'I'm not recording you.'

'It's been two hours since my team arrived at the crime scene. So far, there isn't a single piece of evidence that places a third person in the room at the time of the murder, which leaves only one possible scenario. Elizabeth murdered her assistant, no one else was there that night. The only thing in question is whether it was an accident or intentional. And, if it was intentional, what was her motive?'

'Can I talk to her?'

'No.' Anwar stepped closer to James and looked up at

him. 'I can make no exceptions. Please stay out of this one.' Anwar's dark-brown eyes glared at him.

It was clear that James wasn't getting anywhere with Anwar. There was no way that he would let James interview Elizabeth, even in custody under supervision. *Maybe someone else at the museum could talk about the exhibit.* James sauntered out of the police station, espresso in hand, contemplating his next move.

———

AFTER THE TEN-MINUTE walk from the police station and the anthropology museum, James was once again out of breath. Now, the real work began. It was James's job to tell the slender, grey-haired woman with a pixie cut that one of her curators was in police custody and an Arthurian sword was missing from her museum. As per her introduction, her name was Professor Camilla Watson. She made it clear he was to address her as "Professor." Just another academic with a superiority complex.

'I spoke to Elizabeth Carmichael. Her apartment is a crime scene. She is in police custody for questioning,' James said.

Camilla's face dropped.

'It's a routine police procedure,' James said in an attempt to reassure her. 'I was wondering if you could show me a few pieces from the upcoming Arthurian Exhibit. It'll be a great help for me to see the artefacts for when I write up the story.'

'What's the chief editor doing writing articles for the culture section?' Camilla pushed her black-rimmed glasses up towards the bridge of her nose.

James shifted in his chair. Camilla wrinkled her brow as she angled her body away from him on the other side of her desk. Everything in her office was neat. From her tabletop to the bookshelves, not a single thing was out of place. Her office matched her personality.

She's going to lose it.

James ran through his already prepared monologue, explaining Valentine's absence and giving Camilla just enough information to satisfy, but not too much to evoke further curiosity. He sighed.

'Hmm,' Camilla said. 'You need to learn how to delegate.' Camilla got up from her desk and headed for the door. 'Follow me,' she called over her shoulder as she darted out of her office and down the hall towards a lone door.

Her long fingers glided across the number pad with great precision. She paused. A beep sounded, then the door unlocked.

'Not everything in the museum is real, but this is, and it's the NMA's most expensive piece,' Camilla lectured over her shoulder as she pushed the door open. 'The excavation took six months, and it's been in the museum since the beginning of July.'

A few seconds later, the lights turned on as Camilla entered the room. She froze and stared at the empty glass case. The room was silent apart from a faint hum from the air conditioner.

James stood next to her and placed his arm around her as she turned pale. 'Maybe she's taken it home with her?'

'The sword may have inspired the Arthurian legends and was originally owned by the real King Arthur, the Romano-Britannic leader from the fifth century. It was valued at over five million pounds,' Camilla said with a frantic look in her eye.

'Perhaps it got caught up in the crime scene investigation.'

Camilla's expression hardened at James's words.

'It's not that bad.' James placed his hand on Camilla's shoulder.

'What has she done? What are you not telling me?'

'This is all I know. The police won't release information while the investigation is ongoing.' James backed away from

Camilla. 'However, I have a contact in the police department. And I'm sure he'll release the artefact back to the museum.'

Camilla ran down the hall, towards the office next to hers, with James following. She pulled a pair of keys out of her jacket and opened the door. Once the door flung open, Camilla flicked on the light and stepped inside. She surveyed the room.

'It's missing.'

EIGHT

MONDAY: 11:52 A.M.

LIGHT from the morning sun shone through the sunroof of the holding cell in the Northampton Police Station. Sitting on the cold, blue rubber mattress, Elizabeth stared down the length of the corridor at the phrase printed on the walls in block letters. The phrase was simple and to the point. It read: *Damage the cell = a charge and a court visit!*

As the minutes ticked by, she become more nervous. By now, they'd probably read her file and saw the DVO. She needed a miracle. There was no way the police would let her out. Her life was over. There was a part of her that believed she probably did this, based on her temper and the bruises she left on her husband's face after a night of heavy drinking. The guilt she carried around was unbearable. Then there was the other part of her that was sure her drinking wasn't as bad. She had next to no blackouts and gaps in her memory, apart from last night. *Am I delusional?*

A knock on the door jolted her out of her sea of thoughts and back to the beige walls of the holding cell. The door slowly opened. Standing at the other end of the cell, in the door frame, was a tall man with a head of thick, curly, dark-brown hair with a sprinkling of grey. His dark-brown eyes fixed on her. An uneasy feeling swept over her body. He must have read her file. *It's official, I'm screwed.*

'DCI Anwar Khan,' he said with a nod. 'It's been brought to my attention that you are yet to make your phone call. There's a phone in the hall.' The man gestured into the hall outside, then held the door open for her. *So, he's doing the good cop routine. Understanding, I'm just here to help you.*

Elizabeth took a deep breath as she arose from the rubber mattress then ambled towards the door. As she drew closer it dawned on her, she had no one to call other than Valentine Charlet, a journalist from the culture section at the *Northampton Tribune. Would she help her?*

There was no way she would call Maximilian Nicholls. She didn't trust him. Elizabeth didn't want to call her ex-husband. She could already hear his voice in her mind. The last thing she needed was a lecture—deep down, she knew she had a problem. *I need to clear my name or at least try to find out what really happened before the police.*

Anwar raised his eyebrows at her. 'I'll be waiting just down the hall.'

Elizabeth stepped out of the cell and glanced down the hall. Picking up her pace, she reached for the phone. Over her shoulder, Anwar stood just where he promised. The call was probably monitored and he most likely could hear her every word.

She picked up the receiver and dialled a number on the metal keypad. Listening to the dial tone, her heart raced. The line picked up, and she listened to the greeting from the receptionist at the *Northampton Tribune.* Elizabeth froze. Valentine's phone had been redirected to reception. That wasn't good.

'My name is Elizabeth James. I'm the curator of the Arthurian Exhibit that's due to open at the Northampton Museum of Anthropology. I have an interview with Valentine

Charlet. Can you put me through to her desk? It's super urgent.' Elizabeth's voice broke.

The woman on the other end of the line took a deep breath. 'Unfortunately, Valentine no longer works for the Tribune, but I can put you through to James Lalonde, the chief editor. He's covering your story.'

Elizabeth nodded. 'Okay.'

A few moments later, a thick French accent answered the line.

'Sorry to bother you, but I've been taken into the Northampton Police Station after I called in a crime. My assistant was murdered in my apartment last night while I was sleeping. The police are holding me in a cell. They think I did this. I swear to you, it wasn't me. I didn't do this. This is so embarrassing, but I don't have anyone to turn to.' Tears streamed down Elizabeth's cheeks.

'So, you want me to help clear your name?' James asked with a sense of hesitation lingering in his voice.

'Yes, I wouldn't have called you if I had another option. I'm desperate.'

James paused. 'I'll need to interview you. So, I'll have to find a way to get you released. I'll see what I can do.'

Before she could say another word, the line went dead. Elizabeth stared at the receiver. Now the waiting began. *Hopefully, he can help me. I remember he solved the mystery behind Albert Harrington's death all those years ago.*

NINE

MONDAY: 1:49 P.M.

THE PUNGENT AROMA of burnt Italian coffee beans filled the small inner-city cafe as the barista boiled the milk. A clang sounded when the barista slammed the metal jug on the coffeemaker. James's stomach rumbled. He checked his watch for the third time. It had been less than two hours since Anwar had reluctantly released Elizabeth from the police station's holding cell. Now he knew two things: the police liked Elizabeth for the crime but did not possess evidence to convict, and the murder weapon was possibly missing. She was under suspicion, but James couldn't ask outright. He needed to dance around the topic because angry people don't talk, and the obvious question was bound to upset Elizabeth. And Anwar was fuming. To secure Elizabeth's release, he had to go over his head to the station's super.

A digital chime announced someone entering the front door of Coffee Haven. He looked up.

Thank God.

Elizabeth paused in the doorway and closed her eyes for a moment, then slowly exhaled and surveyed the room. James lifted his hand and waved as she strode towards his table next to the window. Without taking his eyes off her, James tapped the large red button on his smartphone screen and started the recording.

She forced a smile as a crease formed in her brow. 'Look, I don't know or understand how you convinced that man to let me go—'

James shrugged. 'It's not a big deal.'

I only had to burn a bridge I spent the last five years building. All to avoid blank space in the culture section. I'm despicable.

With her hand trembling, Elizabeth reached out and pulled the chair out, then sat. She clenched her trembling hands in her lap and forced a smile.

'Do you want a drink?' James pointed across the room at the coffee bar in the centre of the cafe.

Elizabeth turned and stared out the window. 'I don't drink.'

Not even caffeine?

As he contemplated his next move, James watched Elizabeth's bloodshot eyes glaze over. A few hours earlier, he had listened to the desperation in her voice over the phone and made several assumptions about her. But the woman in front of him was not what he had expected. The insufferable optimist in him had hoped for an easy story. He had become lazy since he took over as editor. Blank space was more important than complicated and sensational news stories. James glanced at his smartphone, laying on the tabletop between him and Elizabeth, and tapped the screen. The numbers on the recording app spun around with military-style precision.

James sighed. 'I know you've been through an ordeal, but walk me through how you discovered the murder.'

'I woke up in my living room.' Elizabeth hesitated as she stared straight through James. 'I must have been exhausted and fell asleep on the couch. I discovered Pippa Baker lying face down on my living room floor. She was dead,' Elizabeth said, all glassy-eyed.

'And you knew this how?' James waited for her reaction.

'I stepped into a pool of her blood. There was no way she could have lost that much blood and survived.'

'And, Pippa, I assume, is your assistant?'

Elizabeth raised her eyebrows.

'I need to be certain of the information I print. So stating the obvious is a part of the job.'

Elizabeth darted her gaze out the window and onto the busy street crammed with pedestrians, buses, and motorists honking their horns in the early afternoon traffic.

James narrowed his eyes. 'Did Pippa stop by your flat the night before?'

'No. When I got home, the house was empty.'

'Where were you the night before?' James rested his chin on the palm of his hand.

'I was in London at a fundraising dinner. I returned late. I can't remember the time, but I'm sure I can find my tickets for the train and cab.'

'Fundraising?'

'Yes, a part of my job as an archaeologist and museum curator is to raise funds for the research that happens after an archaeological dig.'

'So, you're still raising money for Excalibur?'

Elizabeth sighed. 'On my recent dig, I excavated what we believe to be the sword that inspired the legend behind Excalibur.'

'You mentioned the word "we." I'm assuming you're referring to a team?' James watched Elizabeth's slender frame straighten up.

'Yes, that's correct. I had a team of people accompany me on the dig. Mostly staff from the museum and a few experts.'

'And when did you last see the sword?'

'I had taken it home a few weeks ago for further study. I guess they'll have collected it as evidence.'

'The police have possession of a tag bearing a catalogue number. But there's no mention of a sword.'

Elizabeth bit her lower lip as her dark-brown eyes watered. 'It's missing?' She leaned over the table towards James.

'Yes. Could any of your team members have the sword?'

'No, I didn't loan it to anyone and forget.' Elizabeth scowled at him. 'The sword is worth over five million pounds. It's dated back to the correct period, early fourth to the fifth century.' Elizabeth looked at the table and covered her mouth as a tear rolled down her cheek.

Someone deserves an Oscar for best actress.

James crinkled his brow as the waterworks commenced, right on cue.

Why didn't you come clean and tell the police? Why hide the tag?

He looked at his phone's lock screen to see how much time had elapsed since the recording started. 'Earlier you seemed unsure about how you came to be in your living room. Did you have a lot to drink during the fundraising dinner in London?'

Elizabeth leaned back in her chair and scowled at him for a moment. 'Are you accusing me of acting unprofessionally?'

James bit his lip in an attempt to hold back a smile. 'I'm not an idiot. I understand that in order to secure funds from investors that there is usually a bit of wining and dining involved. That's all. You're the one jumping to conclusions. I was wondering what the uncertainty was all about.'

'Of course, you're just wondering,' Elizabeth said with a hint of suspicion lingering in her voice.

James stiffened his posture. 'You called me, remember? You wanted my help. In order to give you that said help, I need to paint a full picture of what happened.'

Elizabeth stared back at him with a blank expression.

'When did you last see Pippa?' James asked as Elizabeth looked towards the counter in the middle of the store.

'Definitely not yesterday.' Elizabeth swallowed hard as she focused on James. 'The day before.'

'So on Saturday.'

'That's what I said.'

'You didn't seem sure, so I wanted to clarify things.' James raised his eyebrows at her.

'Yes,' Elizabeth said with what appeared to be an exasperated shrug.

'Did Pippa have any rivals or enemies?'

'I do not know.' Elizabeth looked up and shrugged again. 'I hope she hasn't done something stupid.'

'Like what?' James leaned back in his chair.

'She was a naïve archaeological graduate with dreams of becoming the next Lara Croft.' Elizabeth shook her head. 'Let's just say that archaeology is far removed from the Indiana Jones and Lara Croft action-adventure films. Maybe she found a private buyer. It would have to be someone wealthy. Extremely wealthy.' Elizabeth stared straight ahead as if she were deep in thought. 'There are strict regulations in the archaeological world. We can't just raid tombs and sell stuff to museums. Everything we find belongs to the country in which we find it.'

'Who would want the sword?'

'No idea. The find isn't public yet. That's why I contacted the culture section of the *Northampton Tribune* and spoke with Valentine. I wanted to draw attention to the exhibit and put the item on display, then raise funds for further research.' Elizabeth waved her hands around. 'Maybe the buyer decided he couldn't trust her.'

'There's no evidence of a third person in your apartment last night.'

'I didn't do it.' Elizabeth furrowed her brow. 'There must be a third person, and that person stole the sword.'

James nodded. 'Okay. I can suspend disbelief for a moment and consider that someone could have been there that night while Pippa was in your flat, while you were sleeping.'

Elizabeth's eyes dilated. 'In the midst of all the drama and gore, I hadn't considered that there were two people walking around my flat while I was sleeping.'

She placed her hand on her mouth and gasped. The colour drained from her face. For the first time, he actually believed her. She was shocked. But there was something Elizabeth wasn't sharing, and it was more than just taking a priceless historical artefact home. She was withholding the truth. It was time to bite the bullet and simply ask the most obvious questions.

James ran his fingers through his thick, dark-blond hair. 'Did you kill your assistant? Even by accident?'

'What?' She jerked back in her chair, then stiffened her posture. 'Have you not listened to a word I've said? I didn't kill Pippa. I...' Elizabeth stuttered as tears rolled down her cheek.

Concerned that he might have pushed her too far, James paused as he watched the tears stream down her cheeks faster than before.

'Sorry, but I have to ask. Why do you think the police were holding you in one of the station's cells? They clearly like you for the crime.' James narrowed his eyes as he gazed across the table.

Elizabeth froze. 'I don't know.'

In an instant the waterworks stopped, and a familiar gaze returned to Elizabeth's dark brown eyes. He had caught her in a third lie. But why lie about the theft of the sword, the drinking, and not knowing why the police thought she killed Pippa?

'All I know is, I didn't do it.' Elizabeth glared at him.

For now, he had to humour Elizabeth and keep her onside.

It was far too soon to be jumping to conclusions. After all, lying was a part of human nature. These false truths might be shared for a multitude of reasons, none of which had anything to do with the murder of Pippa Baker. Or Elizabeth might be trying to cover her tracks.

Then there was the biggest question of all, one that he could never ask. Even if he did, she wouldn't be honest. Why did she call him and not someone from her team?

James leaned across the table toward Elizabeth. 'I think I might agree with you on this. The murderer is most likely the thief. So in theory, if we locate the sword, we'll locate Pippa's murderer too.'

TEN

MONDAY: 3:13 P.M.

AS JAMES KNOCKED on the door of Pippa's studio apartment, a gesture he knew was futile, an older woman in her seventies stuck her head outside the doorframe of the next flat. She was holding a pair of knitting needles.

'Dear, Pippa isn't home. I haven't seen her since yesterday. If you come in, I can make you a cup of tea, and I can call her on her mobile.' She turned around and disappeared into her apartment.

'Okay, that sounds great,' James called from the corridor outside. He followed her into the apartment.

As James stepped inside, he almost tripped over a giant basket full of yarn. To his right, an incomplete patchwork quilt was thrown over the couch. Behind her sofa were rows of shelves crammed full of paperbacks.

'Do you like Earl Grey? Pippa gave me this Extravagant Earl Grey blend from Whittard of Chelsea for my birthday,' the lady said as she filled a small Russell Hobbs cordless kettle, placed it on its base, and flicked the switch.

'When did you last see Pippa?'

'Yesterday afternoon. Pippa was leaving wearing all black. She looked like she was in mourning. I saw her out my front

42

window. I remember I was sitting over there on the couch knitting,' the thin, elderly lady said as she faced James.

'Do you know her well?' He continued to probe, hoping he wouldn't raise her suspicions.

'I suppose. We have tea every day, but not yesterday. She was in a hurry,' the old lady recalled as the kettle whistled away in the background. She poured the hot water into the teapot.

'Was that unusual for her?' James walked across the room towards the small, round kitchen table.

'Who are you, and why are you asking these questions about Pippa?' She shook her finger at him as he took a seat at her kitchen table. 'You better not be a crazy stalker.'

James smiled at the little old lady, who was now standing over him and clutching a red ceramic teapot.

'My name is James Lalonde. I'm the editor of the *Northampton Tribune*. I'm looking for information to help with an investigation.'

'Is Pippa in trouble?'

'I think you should sit down to hear this.'

She shook her finger at him once more. 'Don't you mollycoddle me, young man.'

James grimaced. 'Mollycoddle?'

'You're not from here, are you?' The little old lady nodded to herself. 'You sound French.'

'Yes, I'm from western France. A city called Poitiers.'

She leaned towards him. 'The word first appeared in a Jane Austen novel, and it means you're treating me like a baby.'

'I'm just trying to tell you that what I'm about to say will be upsetting. I'm trying to be kind.'

He gestured towards the seat in front of him. She sat down. The older woman rested the teapot on a giant cork coaster, then looked across the table at James.

'Early this morning, Pippa Baker was found murdered. I'm helping the police to track down her killer by retracing her steps. Anything you could tell me about her would be useful.'

'The police have just left. They weren't interested in talking to me.' The older lady glanced at him with a hint of scepticism in her eyes.

'You caught me. I'm not being entirely honest.' James handed the older lady his card. 'I'm looking into Pippa's death for a contact of mine. They want to know what happened to her.'

'To be honest, I was hoping you were a new suitor, boyfriend, lover, or whatever the kids are calling it these days.' She stared at the card.

'You don't think I'm too old for her?'

'Well, you're younger than the last guy,' she said as James raised his eyebrows at her. 'He must have been at least thirty-five. I think he was American. He had a funny accent.'

'Do you know his name? I want to ask him a few questions.'

'No, she wasn't comfortable talking about her male companions.'

'Did he stay often?'

'He never stayed the night, but he visited frequently. I think he stopped by a week ago.'

James reached into his grey jacket, pulled out his phone, and opened a note. On the screen he typed: *Older boyfriend/lover? 35-ish.*

'Oh, poor Pippa.' The old lady's eyes glazed over as she continued to stare at the card. 'Pippa was American. She went to an expensive university in Massachusetts and had a large debt—she would never pay off that student loan on her current salary.'

'Really?'

'Yes. Pippa was also enrolled in a master's degree programme at the local university. Everything is so expensive these days. I don't know how this generation will survive.'

'Ah, Mrs—'

'Oh, sorry, dear. I'm Pearl Whitehall. But you can call me

Mrs Whitehall. My husband died five years ago. That's why I live alone next to Pippa.'

Mrs Whitehall picked up the teapot and poured James a cup of tea. She placed the teapot down, then she looked up and stared right through him. James looked behind him. There was nothing but an empty corridor.

'Mrs Whitehall, are you remembering something?'

'Oh my. I almost forgot to tell you,' she said as she continued to stare ahead. 'A few hours before Pippa left, that woman from the museum turned up. They had a massive argument. They always argued.'

'Do you remember her name? I need more to go on. Can you describe her to me?'

'It was her boss.' She continued to stare over his shoulder. 'Yes, it was Elizabeth. She was married to that wealthy aristocrat. I think his name was something Carmichael.'

'Did you overhear them?' James pulled out his smartphone and tapped the screen, then he slipped it back into the inside pocket of his jacket.

'Although these walls are thin, the conversation was hard to decipher. They often yelled over the top of each other, and Pippa had that Boston accent. It was often difficult to understand her. You had to listen carefully. But from what I understood, Pippa might have put Elizabeth's research at risk.'

'Oh.' James brushed his hands through his hair.

'Yes, Elizabeth and what's his name?' Mrs Whitehall stared into her tea. 'Alistair,' she said, as she looked up at James.

'Elizabeth's husband was Alistair Carmichael, as in the Alistair Carmichael?'

'You've heard of him?'

'He's obsessed with the Arthurian legend. My grandfather is a fan. I remember he did a book signing and dinner at Pierrefonds. From memory, the book was about Arthurian Mythology, and it mentions the links to Charlemagne and a few other historical figures. My grandfather read the book twice.' James tapped the edge of his teacup, then smiled.

'Well, he and Elizabeth had a bitter divorce, according to Pippa. And they're now rivals.' She leaned in closer towards James. 'They're fighting over some research. And poor Pippa was always caught up in the crossfire. They broke the golden rule of a great marriage.'

'What's that?' He looked up at her.

'Never, ever work with your significant other. Though it worked out well for my Peter and me.'

James nodded to himself as he picked up the cup and took a long sip of his tea. A fruity aftertaste lingered in his mouth as he rested the cup on the kitchen table.

'She was right out there.' Pearl pointed over James's shoulder.

'You mean Elizabeth?' James looked in the direction the old lady had pointed.

'Yes, then two hours later, Pippa left all dressed in black.'

'Have you ever met Elizabeth?'

'No, but from what Pippa told me, she sounded controlling and had a bit of a temper. She was quick to fly off the handle and yell.'

'Thanks, Mrs Whitehall. You've been helpful,' he said as he got up from the table.

'If you have any more questions, feel free to come back and ask.' Mrs Whitehall reached over and tapped the edge of the saucer. 'You should stay and finish your tea. Don't be in such a hurry.'

James glanced at his cup. *A few more minutes won't hurt. And the Carmichael Estate isn't too far away. There's plenty of time before my appointment. Pippa's flat will have to wait.*

'Actually, there is one more thing,' James said as he looked up and stared at the wall between Mrs Whitehall's and Pippa's flats. 'You don't happen to have a key to Pippa's apartment?'

ELEVEN

MONDAY: 5:35 P.M.

THE IVORY-COLOURED GRAVEL crunched under his black Oxford shoes as he walked towards the front door. The front of the house looked more like a miniature summer palace or a museum than a home. But this was where Alistair Carmichael lived. To the left of the driveway was a small English garden with lush green grass, outlined by a hedge that ran up to waist height. James continued walking towards the front door. He knocked, then spun around to soak in the extravagance of the side lawn. There was something familiar about this estate, but he couldn't put his finger on it.

'I know you,' a familiar voice called out from behind him. 'No bodies this time,' the voice added as James turned to see a familiar face standing in front of him.

'I'm a friend of your former...' James thought about the right words to describe their relationship.

'You don't remember me. I guess you remember my former butler with a bat in hand,' Alistair said as he imitated a baseball-style swinging action. 'I bet you remember the missing Van Gogh and one of your journalists face down in my back garden.'

'Yes, that was almost six months ago. My memory is hazy,' James said, 'but the doctor said I might regain some of my memories.'

'Come on in.' Alistair gestured as he walked into the large foyer with James following. 'So, you know my Lizzie?'

'It's more of a new friendship.' James smiled to himself.

His Lizzie. Someone's struggling with reality.

Not that he was in any position to judge.

'Sorry I was late. I got a little lost.'

Alistair shrugged. 'Most people drive straight past the gates.'

James nodded.

'Let's go to the library. It has a better reputation than my garden.' Alistair motioned towards a set of double doors to his left. He walked towards the doors and flung them open.

'How's your lovely lady? I'm surprised she hasn't called already.' Alistair winked at him.

A part of James was a little relieved that he might never receive another one of those calls, but then there was the other part, the one that longed for Valentine to call and scream at him about how he was spending too much time at work or was late getting home for dinner.

'She left me,' James said, hoping the questions would cease.

'Yes, they have a habit of doing that.' Alistair walked across the library towards the armchair closest to the bookcase. 'Would you like a drink?' He pointed towards the drink cart tucked away near the doors.

'No, thanks.' James paused at the doorway and stared at the cart, jam-packed with numerous types of liquor and tumblers. 'I've got a lot on my plate at work.'

'Suit yourself.'

'Elizabeth is mixed up in something, and I'm trying to clear her name.' James walked around to the other side of the couch and sat down.

'Really?' Alistair sat down as well and stroked the fabric on his armchair.

'Yes, she woke up this morning to find her assistant, Pippa Baker, had died during the night in her living room.'

'Not Pippa.' Alistair leaned forward, rested his elbow on the arm of the chair, and propped up his head. 'She was such a hardworking and passionate student of archaeology. That's a real shame.'

'I want to ask a few questions about Pippa, Elizabeth, archaeology, and maybe how all of this works.' James pulled out his phone and pressed the record button. 'Do you mind?'

Alistair shook his head.

'So, do you fund your archaeological digs?'

Alistair leaned forward towards James. 'No, I did when I was younger and more carefree. Archaeology is a tough business—and an expensive one. Now we have corporate sponsors and work for private buyers on the rare occasion.'

'We?'

'I work with Maximilian Nicholls. He's my business partner.'

'And the private buyers?'

'The private buyers will loan these items to museums. That's how they make money. It's not right, but you also need to make money, so compromises need to be made. It's the only way you can make a decent living in this industry.' Alistair looked across the room at the wall of mahogany-stained bookshelves packed with cloth-covered hardback books from a bygone era.

'And Elizabeth? Do you know how she finances her digs?'

'Yes, I do. The dig started about fourteen months ago. We've been researching the real-life king and artefacts that inspired the Arthurian legends. Our team excavated the sword that inspired the legend behind Excalibur.'

'You excavated this?' James asked.

'Lizzie found it. I helped her remove it after she discovered it. I would never dream of taking credit for any of her discoveries.' Alistair leaned back in his chair and shook his index finger.

James smirked as he glanced at the antique furniture that lined the sitting room. 'So, back to Elizabeth and her funding?'

'Elizabeth is an idealist and a passionate dreamer. She's opinionated, especially in regard to corporate funding and private buyers. Elizabeth believes the artefacts belong to the country of origin. I'm sure she thinks I'm a sell-out.' Alistair shrugged. 'Elizabeth still fundraises the old-fashioned way, wining and dining to secure grants from governments, universities, and museums. It's difficult. And I'd imagine that she is in a considerable amount of debt.'

James narrowed his eyes. 'So, you're saying that she funds the dig herself?'

Alistair shifted in his chair. 'We faced a few issues getting started with the dig. The Cornwall council wasn't cooperating, so we got the Northampton Museum of Anthropology involved, and they partially funded the dig. Their money and help with the council came at a price: for the sword to be on permanent display in their museum.' Alistair tapped the arm of his chair. 'But we still didn't have enough money. So, Elizabeth turned to government grants, universities, and then she caved with the first private investor she found; someone who is still anonymous to this day, no less. I think that was Elizabeth's personal money. She also sold her mortgaged property around the same time. I got a friend involved. He introduced us to other minor investors and one major player who wants to remain anonymous.'

James pursed his lips. 'And all these investors agree the sword should stay in the museum? No one wants it to be a part of their own private exhibit?'

Alistair laughed. 'Who do you think invested in the dig?

Bruce Wayne? Don't be ridiculous. These people invest in these things all the time. They know what they're getting themselves into.'

————

THE SLAMMING of a door echoed through the foyer and into the sitting room. Alistair looked over James's shoulder and smiled, then waved. James turned around to see an intimidating tower of muscle walking towards them. It was a man in his mid-thirties with chiselled cheekbones and sparkling blue eyes.

'This is my business partner, Maximilian Nicholls.' Alistair stood up and patted Maximilian on the back.

James nodded as the two men sat down in the armchairs opposite him.

'We were just talking about your favourite person,' Alistair said.

Maximilian forced a smile as he tapped his fingers on the arm of the couch and shot a glassy stare in James's direction.

'Not a fan?' James stared at the pink cut across Maximilian's cheek, the only flaw on his perfectly sculpted face.

'She's difficult.' Maximilian clutched his hands as he looked across at the bookshelves, avoiding James's gaze.

James squinted as he evaluated the man sitting opposite him. 'Stubborn, not difficult.'

'She works as the curator of the NMA. We had the great pleasure of going on a dig with her and Pippa about fourteen months ago. Unfortunately, we're still researching and collecting data, but it's looking promising.' Maximilian looked at James and narrowed his eyes.

James paused for a moment and soaked up Maximilian's disdain for Elizabeth.

'The only way to make more money from this dig is to publish findings. We need to work together in peace,' Alistair explained to James.

'Why are you here?' Maximilian asked James. 'Are you doing a piece on our dig? I don't recall seeing that in my calendar.'

'I'm here on behalf of Elizabeth. She found Pippa Baker dead in her living room this morning. So far, Elizabeth is the only suspect.' James made eye contact with Maximilian.

'That's unfortunate.' Maximilian looked over James's shoulder and stared into the foyer behind him.

'I want to help clear her name.'

'You don't think she could have done it?' Maximilian raised his eyebrows at James. 'Even by accident?'

'What are you saying?' Alistair asked.

'Elizabeth has a temper.' Maximilian pointed at Alistair.

'She's never hit anyone.' Alistair tilted his head to the side and grimaced at Maximilian.

'What about Pippa? Do you think she could have gotten herself into some trouble?' James glanced back and forth between the two men sitting in front of him.

'Pippa is an American undergraduate with no connections, money, or experience. It's unlikely that she could find trouble,' Maximilian said.

'You seem to know her well.'

'Of course he does. We both do. Pippa was on the dig with us. I still can't believe Elizabeth hired a student with zero experience,' Alistair said.

Maximilian shrugged and frowned. 'She wasn't that bad. She was hardworking and did what was necessary.'

He seems to be a huge fan. Interesting.

'I know you're looking for drama, something scandalous about your next headline. I guess you can't help it. But there's none here other than theft and murder.' Maximilian's icy gaze fixed on James. 'I know these women well. After all, I spent months on an excavation with both of them. Pippa was hardworking, and Elizabeth has a feisty side. If you don't believe me, poke the bear. I dare you. It's your funeral.'

Alistair patted Maximilian on the back. 'He's just trying to get a sense of things, Max. No need to get all worked up, ol' chap.'

TWELVE

JAMES PULLED over to the side of the road and turned the key. As the engine of his Peugeot came to a halt, James pulled his phone off the charging holder and started typing away. He needed to capture this idea before he lost his train of thought. James had so much to do that he no longer trusted his ability to remember an idea.

He hesitated, then flicked the incoming notifications off the screen.

Was there something more concrete behind the mud-slinging matches between the three archaeologists?

He was certain that no one was telling the truth. Everyone had something to hide, something they weren't telling him, a secret he had to find out for himself.

As he contemplated the possibilities, his heart raced. James leaned over his steering wheel and continued typing in the notes app on his phone. This was what was missing from his career—the thrill of chasing a story. But he had to put that on hold for now. He had a newspaper to attend to and neglecting his editorial position would put his career in jeopardy. As he pictured Harry Lancaster's angry, wrinkled face upon the report of a missed print-run deadline, a familiar shape caught his eye.

He dropped his smartphone on the passenger seat, leaned forward, and stared out the window. James took a deep breath as he continued to gaze at the familiar Mini parked on the side of the road a few metres down from the hotel. A lump formed in his throat.

I thought she was leaving for Paris.

James picked up his phone and scrolled through his directory. Even with his glasses on, he struggled to read the letters imprinted on the number plate. His heart started beating faster.

It's her car.

He looked down at the information on his screen.

Something within him wanted to race across the road to the hotel and beg her to take him back. A sharp pain shot through his chest as he unbuckled his seat belt and slipped the keys into his pocket. He grabbed the door handle and sighed.

What would he say to her? He had no excuses or eloquent words. Valentine had made her choice. As much as he wanted to kiss and make up and win her back, he knew there was no changing her mind. James had to respect her decision to leave. He realised a part of him would do almost anything to get her back.

Was this how Alistair felt about Elizabeth? Did he do something unspeakable to get the woman he loved to run to him in a time of crisis?

James pulled out the keys from his pocket and slipped them back into the ignition. A hard lump formed in his throat as he imagined Valentine packing her suitcase and then boarding a train to London, St Pancras. He was never going to see her again.

THIRTEEN

MONDAY: 7:07 P.M.

A FLOWERY AROMA burst through the ajar front door as James pulled the key he had received from Mrs Whitehall out of the lock. The police must have dismissed her as a nosy old woman with nothing new to share. James wrinkled his nose and held his breath as the piquant fragrance intensified. The door swung open to reveal Pippa's pristine white studio apartment, now dusted in fingerprint powder. Neat was an understatement. It didn't do the sight justice. Her tiny, minimalist apartment was picturesque, like it belonged in those home living magazines that Valentine obsessed over.

The ivory two-seater sofa with rounded arms, lined with small grey cushions, was positioned in the centre along the left wall. To its far left was a white four-door wardrobe followed by a small white bedside table, and a double bed pushed up against the radiator mounted on the right wall. It was definitely a place for one.

James closed the door behind him and took a few steps. He found himself in the centre of the room. And that's when he saw it. A lone white candle sat in the centre of the radiator's cover, next to a 100ml glass bottle of Miss Dior. Squinting, James leaned forward to get a closer look at the bottle.

That's the eau de parfum. How can she afford that?

James walked over to the radiator, picked up the small silver lid and placed it on top of the Jo Malone orange blossom candle. As his eyes wandered over to the perfume bottle, a deep sense of curiosity developed within him. The floorboards creaked underneath his shoes as he strolled towards the wardrobe. Inside was a rack packed to the brim with high street clothes, not a single designer item in sight. He closed the door and turned around.

Interesting.

The walnut-stained dining table turned desk was pushed up against the wall where the flatscreen TV hung. And to the right was a tall walnut-stained coatrack bearing a men's plaid jacket. It was the only hint of the presence of a man in the entire flat. James walked over to the coatrack and lifted the jacket off the hook. He brushed his hand along the plaid material—it felt expensive. He turned the jacket around to inspect the tag.

It's bespoke.

James held the plaid jacket in the air by its shoulders. *It's got to be a 3XL.* Was it left before or after the crime scene team did a sweep?

A deep furrow appeared on his brow as James carefully lifted the jacket back onto its hook. He ambled over to the kitchen door and peered through the small window. Out of the corner of his eye, James spotted a MagSafe cord protruding between the table and the wall.

Great, Anwar has her laptop.

Reaching out, James pulled a chair out from the table as a purple and white spotted pen rolled onto the floor and under the double bed.

Merde.

Crouching on the floor, James peeped under the bed. A large piece of shimmering metal plated in gold lay undisturbed

—forgotten. *Or was it planted after the police visited Pippa's flat?*

James crawled closer and reached out towards the mysterious gold object. As his hand struck the cool metal, James realised it was a laptop. Ignoring the pen, James pulled the computer closer to him and stood up. Upon opening the laptop, a chime followed by a click broke the silence of the apartment. She didn't have a password. The screen opened to reveal an open email in the computer's default mail system. Possibly the last email she had ever read. It was from Elizabeth, telling Pippa not to do any more podcast interviews without her consent. At that moment, James knew he couldn't keep this to himself any longer.

FOURTEEN

A SHORT, sharp knock jolted James back to reality. He looked up over his computer screen to find Josh from Layout at his office door.

I must have dozed off.

James stretched out the tight muscles at the back of his neck. A digital typewriter sound shrieked out of his phone. He grimaced. It was a ringtone reserved for one person, Owen Swift, a friend from his days at All Saints College. And his timing was eerily poetic. *What now?* Against his better judgement, James reached out and tapped the screen. Owen had sent a picture. On the surface, it seemed like a normal gesture. But this was Owen—nothing was ever normal with him. As the image loaded on the screen, the façade of the New York Public Library came into view. James rolled his eyes as the caption appeared. It read: *Wish you were here.*

Work commitments stood in the way of James attending the boy's extra-long weekend away. So naturally, Owen was punishing him with images of events he missed out on—this morning, it was a series of pictures from five different pubs. Tonight, it was a library he dreamed of visiting. James turned his smartphone over. He was not texting Owen back. For weeks, he had meant to text his best friend, Liam, but work had gotten in the way again. It was taking over his life.

'It's ready. I made the changes. I tried to get it done as fast as possible,' Josh said as he approached James's desk.

James double-clicked on InDesign and started searching for the edition of the story he had looked over an hour earlier.

'I should be a few minutes.' James fixed his eyes on the screen, reached towards his top desk drawer, pulled out his glasses, and put them on. There was no use denying it. The closer he got to thirty, the more he needed to wear them.

James scrolled through the file, pausing every now and then. It was finally perfect. 'Go for it. Get it ready for Impression. We're already behind schedule.' James closed the programme on his screen.

'It's cool. We can still make midnight.' Josh backed away and scurried down the hall.

'I want to see the first copy,' James said as his eyes wandered over to the tiny digital clock at the top right-hand corner of his screen. It read 11:15 p.m. and, in two more hours, he could return home. He couldn't let himself leave if his journalists were still working past a deadline. And tonight was one of those nights.

This is why she left me.

TEN MINUTES EARLIER, James passed the Queens Head pub on the way home. Perhaps out of a need to drown his sorrows at the dumpster fire that resembled his life, he ambled through its front door. A group of locals leaned against the dark-brown wooden bar and craned their necks to look up at the results from the Hull vs Arsenal game from earlier that day while keeping one eye on the bartender. James rolled his eyes. He could never understand their obsession with football. Rugby, he could understand, but football was boring. He looked at the empty pint in his hands as he contemplated another.

He glanced at the antique clock above the bar, and a familiar short Malaysian man leaned over and pointed at something behind the bartender. James smiled.

One more drink.

James arose from his stool, walked towards the bar, and pushed through a small group of people who were staring at the specials on the chalkboard above. He placed his hand on Chan's shoulder. Chan jumped, then swayed a little from side to side. The off-duty police constable reached over, grabbed the bar, and steadied himself.

'Having a good night, David?' James asked with a hint of a chuckle in his voice.

'Call me Chan. Everyone else does,' Chan slurred as he pointed towards James. 'I shouldn't be talking to you.'

'You need to ask Anwar's permission to do that?'

'He reminded me that you have a nose for trouble and a front page to fill.'

'Ouch.' James raised his glass at the bartender. 'I'm paying,' he said as he tilted his head towards Chan.

Chan looked up at James as if he was contemplating his next move, then raised his finger. He smirked. 'Forgot what I was going to say.'

'When did you and Anwar get married?'

'Very funny.'

'He sounds more like an overbearing wife than a boss. You know, checking in at home before you do things, constantly asking for permission.'

'That's Anwar.'

'He used to be a lot of fun.'

'Really?' Chan leaned in towards James and took a sip of his beer.

'That was before his big promotion, marriage, and the little one on the way.'

'Yeah, he's no barrel of laughs at work either.'

James handed his credit card over to the bartender and smiled.

'No.' Chan hunched over the bar and shook his head.

'Let's just take a table and chat for a few minutes. Five at the most.'

'I can't.'

'You need Anwar's permission to do the right thing? We both know that you and Anwar arrested the wrong person today. It was convenient,' James said as he observed Chan's reaction.

The PC sighed and looked at the floor.

He knows.

'You're just after information.' Chan picked his pint off the bar and walked towards a pair of stools perched against a tall wooden table adjacent to the bar.

James raised his eyebrows as Chan staggered towards the first chair.

Someone's a bit of a lightweight.

'The sword is missing from the NMA, and Elizabeth has confessed to me that she took it home the night of the murder,' James said as Chan sat down on the first stool.

'She never mentioned that during the interview.'

'I wonder what else she didn't mention during your interview.' James sipped his beer and took a seat next to the PC.

'I can't do this. If Anwar finds out about this conversation, I'm toast.' Chan stared at his glass.

'All I'm asking is to share what we know. This is clearly more than a murder. That sword was the real reason the suspect was in her apartment that night, and the murder was just something that happened.'

'And Pippa just happened to be in Elizabeth's apartment that night?' Chan put his beer on the table.

'Maybe she was in her apartment for the sword or was working late at night in Elizabeth's office. It's hard to say.'

'I can't do this.' Chan got up off his stool. 'Thanks for the beer.'

Chan drank the rest of his pint, slammed it down on the table, and turned to walk away.

'I found a custom-made plaid jacket in Pippa's apartment today.' James took a sip of his beer and continued to stare straight ahead.

Chan sighed, reached over, and grabbed the empty beer off the table. 'Expensive.'

'It belongs to a large-framed individual. It's at least a 3XL.' James turned around and raised his eyebrows at Chan.

'Your point?'

'Maximilian's a big guy. How much do you think he weighs? At least two hundred pounds?'

Chan released his grip on the beer and pointed his index finger at James. 'Talking to you was a mistake.'

'But that's not all I found.' James sipped his beer.

Chan sighed. 'You found nothing of consequence in that flat. My team and I combed that place over.'

James shrugged. 'Well, you either missed Pippa's laptop hidden under her bed, or someone returned to the flat after you were done and left it to be discovered later.'

'No, I'm not falling for this.' Chan shook his finger.

'Imagine how it would look if a PC solved a crime that a DCI missed?'

Chan paused for a moment. He shook his head and turned around.

'You could check Pippa's and Maximilian's phone records or email. And have a chat with her neighbour, Pearl Whitehall.' James shrugged. 'It wouldn't hurt.'

Chan turned around and glared at James. 'What's in this for you?'

'There's a story here. A great one. One worthy of a front

page.' James stood up and walked towards Chan. 'My question for you is, which headline would you prefer? Wrongful arrest, or the one where you're named as the arresting officer? Or you can do what Anwar says, knowing deep down it's the wrong thing,' James said in a hushed tone.

Chan sighed and stared at the empty glass on the table. He grabbed the glass and looked up at James.

'The next one is on me.'

FIFTEEN

TUESDAY: 1:59 A.M.

JAMES STAGGERED through the front door and walked towards the light coming from the kitchen. He paused.

Did I leave that on?

He didn't hear a single sound within his maisonette. He was definitely alone. The clock struck twice as James walked to the kitchen and dropped his bag on the table.

Food or sleep. That was the only decision that awaited him. Despite how hungry he was, the thought of rest was far more inviting. As he turned towards the staircase, out of the corner of his eye, he caught sight of a black plastic knife handle protruding from the refrigerator door.

Oh, great. Another break-in.

James walked to the refrigerator. His chest tightened as he inhaled. The light was on for a reason.

James stared at the horror laid out before him. Someone perfectly positioned the knife at eye level. A polished metal blade pinned a picture and a note to the door. The message was on a piece of plain white printing paper. It consisted of different-coloured letters, likely cut out of various magazines and journals. He didn't bother reading it.

He didn't need to. The picture said it all.

With his trembling hands, he pulled the note and picture off the fridge. As a journalist, James had received his fair share of death threats and the odd trashing of his house. All were designed to evoke fear. They all wanted one thing—for him to drop a story and stop chasing a lead. The tactics had never been successful until now.

This time, it was different.

James took a few steps back and rested his body against the kitchen counter behind him. As he continued to stare at the image of Valentine gagged and slumped against a metal chair in an empty room, his legs gave out. His back slid down the doors of the kitchen counter, and his body crashed onto the cold tiles. He placed his hand over his mouth and sobbed. Through the sea of tears, he read the top line of text.

Let it go, or I'll finish what I started. I'll be in touch.

SIXTEEN

TUESDAY: 7:02 A.M.

JAMES WALKED through the first floor of the Northampton Museum of Anthropology and up the staircase to the upper level.

Did I make the right decision? Should I have mentioned this to Anwar?

He followed the platform around and passed a series of lecture halls until he came to a corridor. James took a deep breath.

Whoever kidnapped Valentine murdered Pippa and stole the sword.

James marched down the hall towards the door labelled "Elizabeth James." He was sure he had already met the murderer, thief, and kidnapper. James had everything he needed, a short list of suspects, and a very personal motivation. They had used a certain personal pronoun, so he was looking for one individual.

He knocked on the closed door. The dull thud of a pair of heels clacking against the floor came from within the office. The handle turned, and the door opened.

'We need to talk.' James pushed past Elizabeth, who was wearing the same outfit from the day before.

He walked across the room and sat down on the chair on the other side of Elizabeth's desk. She turned around and stared at him.

'I'm pretty sure I've told you everything I know about the events that unfolded.' Elizabeth took a deep breath.

'See, that's where you and I disagree. I have a hunch there's a lot more to tell.' James leaned back in the chair and held her gaze.

Elizabeth gestured towards the door and down the corridor. 'I don't respond to intimidation tactics.'

Her slender frame tensed as he remained seated.

'Do you want me to come back with PC Chan? I can always let him off his leash and see what happens.' James crossed his legs, then brushed a small piece of fluff off his arm and refocused on Elizabeth. 'Or you can take a seat and have an honest chat with me.'

Elizabeth stood clutching the door handle and looked down the hall. She closed the door behind her, walked across the room, and sat down at her desk.

'He's just a bobby.' Elizabeth refocused her attention on James. 'He doesn't scare me.'

James raised his eyebrows at her.

'I don't know what you expect me to say,' Elizabeth said, avoiding James's gaze.

'How about we start with the small mountain of debt you've racked up in the pursuit of a legendary sword?' James brushed his hand along his trouser leg, then looked up at her.

'I guess I can assume because you're here asking me you have no factual evidence and what you know is merely a work of fiction.' Elizabeth scowled at him with her chocolate-brown eyes.

'So, what you're saying is if I ask PC Chan for a warrant and we seize all of your company's records, we'll find that you're well in the green.' James tilted his head towards the door and smirked.

'I made a mistake asking you for help. So I guess that front page of your low-circulation newspaper is looking more like a gossip rag and you're desperate for a decent story to save your arse.'

James smirked. 'Oh, really?'

'Yes, I've met Harry Lancaster.'

'That's nice.' James pulled out his smartphone and started typing away at the screen.

'That's all you have?' Elizabeth stood up at her desk and leaned towards him. 'You're here to intimidate me and accuse me of dishonesty and verging on bankruptcy, all on a whim?' She struck her desk with her index finger.

James looked up and smiled.

'Bear with me, Mrs Carmichael. I'm just emailing PC Chan. I need to give him time to request a search warrant. The police are funny about paperwork and procedure.' James refocused on his screen.

'You're not the only one who's done a bit of research.'

James glanced up at Elizabeth and bit his lower lip in an attempt to stop himself from smiling.

'Yes, I know all about you. You're just some twelve-year-old in an editorial position who has a trust fund, time on your hands, and money to burn.'

'I think I'm developing a crush on you. I love a woman who does her research.' James placed his hand on his chest.

'God, you're just like Alistair,' Elizabeth said in a sharp tone as she sat.

'For the record, I'm almost twenty-nine, and the last time I checked, I wasn't the editor of the *Times*. The *Tribune* is a small newspaper with a small circulation. And yes, I went to Oxford.' James looked down and continued to type. 'Not that it's any of your business, but I inherited some money a few years back. I was raised to work hard, not live off the wealth of another. It's not my money. I didn't earn it.'

Elizabeth sighed. 'You can stop typing.'

James looked up from his phone and raised his eyebrows. 'A sudden change of heart?'

'Do you want to hear what I have to say?' Elizabeth leaned forward and narrowed her eyes at him.

'Enlighten me.' James pushed his glasses up on the bridge of his nose.

'You're right.'

James reached across and placed his phone on the desk. 'You're going bankrupt?' He leaned forward.

'I'm in archaeology for the love of it. I've always dreamed about excavating lost treasures and discovering lost civilisations. But it's an expensive business, and I'm in a considerable amount of debt.'

James leaned back and listened to her confession. 'Go on,' he said as Elizabeth's gaze flicked upwards.

'I've considered breaking a few laws to sell off the sword to pay for debts, but I decided against it because that would be career suicide. I've got too much to lose. And I certainly wouldn't have involved Pippa.' A hint of sadness lingered in Elizabeth's voice.

'What do you mean by career suicide?'

'If I don't find the sword and return it to the NMA, my career and reputation will be ruined. No one in the archaeological world would ever work with me again.'

'I know you're working with Alistair and Maximilian. I can imagine the fallout from an event like this wouldn't be as bad as you're letting on. Why have you not mentioned your partnership with them?' James sat up straight in his chair.

'Alistair and Maximilian are corporate sell-outs. The museum gave me partial funding, and I was desperate. They have funds, and I knew Alistair would jump at anything Arthurian.' Elizabeth ran her finger through a pile of sticky notes.

'Fair enough. What about your rocky relationship with Pippa?'

'I didn't kill Pippa. She drove me insane and put my research in jeopardy a few times, but she made me a better professional.'

'How did she put your research in jeopardy?'

'It wasn't intentional, but she talked about the discovery on her blog. It was more like a diary update. When I found it, I asked her to take it down.'

'That's it?' James pushed his glasses back up. 'She blogged about it to an audience of zero people?'

'She caused a fight on the dig site between Alistair and Maximilian. I don't want to get into it.' Elizabeth shuffled around in her chair.

'I do. It's important. If the police find out about this, then it's another piece of evidence that makes you look guilty.'

'Pippa did a few podcast interviews about the dig, and our research, as well. At that stage, we didn't need press. Her actions made the investors uncomfortable.'

'Like who?'

'I can't say because he specifically requested to remain anonymous. He's quite an affluent individual who likes to keep his financials private.'

Elizabeth tucked her hair behind her ears, picked up the pile of sticky notes on her desk, and flipped through them.

'Off the record?'

'I can't.'

James ran his fingers through his thick blond hair and stared at the woman in front of him. He had a lot of work to do, and time was slipping away.

'I know you saw Pippa the day of the murder. That afternoon at her flat. Multiple witnesses overheard your conversation with her.'

Elizabeth laughed. 'You're referring to that interfering busybody who lives next door?'

James smirked. 'Yes, Elizabeth, I regularly take the word of one individual and don't check multiple sources. You caught me.'

'Like who?'

'I will not reveal my sources. It's unethical.' James removed his spectacles and held them as he glanced across the room at Elizabeth.

'So, you do have standards.'

James shook his head. 'You asked for my help. Remember?'

They sat in silence, staring at each other as James contemplated his next move.

SEVENTEEN

A THICK LAYER of haze distorted her vision of the room as she slowly opened her eyes. The tiny hairs on her arms stood on end. As she tried to hunch over and protect herself from her new cold climate, a stinging sensation shot across her wrists. She couldn't move. It was as if she were attempting to wake herself out of a dream. She looked down. Her heart raced as she realised her nightmare. She was bound to a chair. The coolness of the thick, coarse rope plunged into her skin as she continued to twist.

How did I get here?

She continued to strain forward. The last thing she could remember was waking up in her hotel room alone. Wrestling against her bonds, she felt the polished wood of the chair brush against her skin, causing the pores to form goose bumps. The room felt like a fridge. She peered down at her bonds once more. Where her rose-gold watch once lay was an indent tattooed onto her skin.

She felt terrible because she had just left the man she loved and admitted defeat. There was no use pretending or hoping things would change. The kind and playful man that she fell in love with had morphed into a workaholic who showed no signs of slowing down or changing. He lived for his job, and it was demanding. It followed him home and consumed their weekends. Her partner had slowly morphed into a roommate. And she was left to vie for his attention, hoping he would hear her voice amongst the sea of many others.

Although she was proud of him and everything he'd achieved, she knew he would never change. He was an optimist, a hopeless romantic, and would always hold on and never let go. She loved him, but this was not the relationship she wanted. Three years after they'd first met, she found herself all alone in a strange city and facing a terrible decision. But she didn't want to be the woman who pressured her man to give up a career he loved.

So she left. Now she was all alone in a dimly lit basement somewhere, knowing that she had broken his heart and he would never know to look for her. After all, she'd made it perfectly clear that she was returning to Paris and didn't want him to follow her.

A sharp pain shot through Valentine's head as her vision became a little clearer. She looked down at the thick, dark-red rings around her wrists. Over to the far right-hand side of the room were rows of shelves lined with stone jars, all bearing a thick layer of dust.

I must be in a warehouse.

Valentine leaned forward to loosen the rope that bound her to the chair. She paused and squinted into the darkness that lay ahead of her. For the first time since she woke up, a faint outline of a person appeared to be standing in the shadows. Something within her knew they had been watching the entire time.

Valentine pushed her tongue into her gag and tried to push it farther down her face as her heart raced. But it was no use. She wasn't going anywhere. Valentine inched forward, and her skin burned as the rope dug into her.

'What do you want from me?' she asked, muffled by the

gag. She attempted to lean forward to get a closer look at the person in the shadows.

The figure remained silent. An eerie sensation swept over Valentine as the silence continued. If intimidation was the game they were playing, it was working. *But why? Why am I down here?*

EIGHTEEN

A WALL of tagged treasures from another world, all of them lined with dust, stood behind Elizabeth like an army looking down and waiting to pounce. Elizabeth took a few deep breaths as James waited for the answer to his question.

'If that's true, then you probably know why I didn't mention my meeting with Pippa,' Elizabeth said as a tear rolled down her cheek. 'I had a fight with her the day she was murdered. I feel guilty because the last thing I said to her was out of anger. And that detective and your PC friend both think I'm suspect number one.'

She wiped away a tear from her big brown eyes and looked at him from across the desk. 'I didn't do it. I didn't murder Pippa, and I did not sell off the sword.'

James smiled at her sympathetically and crinkled his brow, unsure how to ask the next question and the one after that.

There was definitely a third person present that night.

James continued to stare at the shelves behind her.

'Some of them are forgeries.' Elizabeth looked at the shelves behind her, interrupting his train of thought.

'Why do you keep them here?'

'I specialise in anthropology. They fascinate me.'

He paused, then tapped the screen of his phone. James sighed. Pippa must have been stealing the sword for someone, and things took an unexpected turn. James looked up at Elizabeth and composed himself for the next questions and the inevitable pushback.

'I don't mean to be indelicate, but can we circle back to the infamous Mr Carmichael?' James politely smiled at Elizabeth.

She shrugged and bit the inside of her lip as a pained expression swept across her face, then disappeared a moment later. 'I guess,' she said in a hushed tone.

'What do you know about Alistair's company? I'm guessing you must have looked into it before accepting his funds.' James leaned forward in his chair and knocked his knees on the back wooden panel of her desk.

'I guess I could bore you with the legal structure and his funding, but I gather that's not what you're after,' Elizabeth said. 'I'm not entirely aware, but knowing Alistair, he doesn't take care of the business aspect of it. He doesn't care for it, nor does he have the aptitude.'

'Yes, he strikes me as the absentminded professor type.' James rubbed his right knee. 'I gather that's what the six-foot blue-eyed muscle does?'

Elizabeth laughed. 'Yes, that's the impression I get as well. He must be the one who secures the corporate sponsors.'

'Is he an accountant?' James asked.

'Have you not heard of Maximilian Nicholls?' Elizabeth raised her eyebrows at him and tilted her head towards the rows of filing boxes to her right.

James shrugged, rested his elbows on the edge of her desk, and propped up his chin.

'He's earned himself quite the reputation in the archaeological world. Maximilian is considered a looter for hire and has a vast network of connections. I think that is why he plays a research-and-business role in Alistair's company. Or it could be a PR thing.'

'Wait? You mean like a tomb raider?'

'Yes. It was challenging to get him access to the dig site. Many of the more respected investors, like the NMA, were a little uneasy and had concerns.' Elizabeth shook her head.

'Why go to all the trouble?' James narrowed his eyes and ran his finger around the edge of her desk lamp.

'Alistair insisted he needed Maximilian.'

'Really?'

'Yes, and he came in handy at the end.'

James leaned back in his chair and looked across at the woman in front of him. 'How?'

Elizabeth sighed. 'It's a long story, but there was a bit of sabotage from a rival. He's a bit of a brute. But everything worked out in the end.'

How was someone able to murder Pippa with no sign of a struggle, steal the sword, and leave completely undetected?

Elizabeth relaxed into her chair. He wanted to believe that Elizabeth was telling the truth, but she had a motive for killing Pippa. So did a few others. All James knew for sure was he needed to keep a close eye on Elizabeth now that she was no longer on edge. James looked across at her and smiled.

NINETEEN

TUESDAY: 9:12 A.M.

ELIZABETH LOOKED AT HER WATCH. It was twelve minutes past nine in the morning, and she had just agreed to accompany that trust-fund-kid-turned-editor all the way to London.

I'm sure I didn't kill her. I would remember that, right? My alcohol consumption is under control. I'm not that woman anymore.

She darted up the path towards the street leading to her apartment complex. For the first time this year it was warm and the sun was out, but it was still cool enough for her to wear her trench coat. It was her favourite time of year. After what seemed like the longest winter, it was nice to see the sun again. As she continued to race up the footpath, a shadow hovered over her.

She looked over her shoulder to find a white panel van rolling down the road at a glacial pace. Elizabeth pulled out her phone and picked up her stride.

The speed limit in the area had recently been reduced to twenty because of the roadworks, but the van had to be doing less than that. She focused her attention down the road ahead of her. The traffic was fine. She looked into the reflection created by her darkened smartphone screen. The van was still crawling along the road. Elizabeth hit the home button, brought up the dial pad, and acted as if she had the worst reception in the world and was trying to make a call.

It certainly wasn't a stretch. Great coverage was not something the phone companies had mastered in this part of Northampton. She squinted at her reflection in the screen and tilted it so she could see the driver. All she could see was another man-child in a purple hoodie. Elizabeth pulled her phone to her ear and sighed.

I must be paranoid. There's no way someone would be following me like this in broad daylight.

She hit the power-saving button and slipped the phone into her pocket, then continued to dart up the footpath. As Elizabeth got closer to her street, her mind wandered. She blinked back the tears that were welling up in her eyes—the last thing she needed was to be seen crying in public. The events of the last week were taking a toll. Right now, she needed to focus all her waking hours on finding the sword. Any day now, Camilla was going to drag Elizabeth into her office and fire her, but for now she believed the sword was in police custody. All she needed was an investor to rock up and request to see the piece. After that, everything would be over. Camilla would discover her lie. Next, her life would comprise of court cases, legal fees, and worst of all, prison. Her heart raced and her chest tightened as she contemplated this potential reality.

Will I be able to find work again? What am I going to move on to if my archaeological career goes up in smoke?

As she turned the corner and walked down her street towards the pedestrian gate of her apartment complex, she paused and looked over her shoulder. No one was around.

It was definitely paranoia.

———

ELIZABETH WALKED up the hall of her apartment. She stopped at the doorway leading to her living room.

Did I really drink that much?

She stared at the bloodstain in the middle of the floor. The atmosphere of the apartment was different. It had been disturbed. This once safe and comforting place was more like an exhibit out of a crime-and-punishment museum than a retreat from the chaos of the outside world.

Was I so drunk that I don't remember committing a crime? She squeezed her eyes shut, blocking out the nightmarish world around her. It had been almost two years since she woke up that fateful day with the mother of all hangovers to discover that she had beaten her husband in a fit of rage and damaged various Carmichael heirlooms. The evidence had spoken for itself. And then there were the bruises on Alistair's face and the faint bruises on her knuckles. She opened her eyes and placed her hand over her mouth as she stared at the bloodstain. *I've done it again.*

She tiptoed through the living room towards the bay window behind her modular sofa. She paused. A familiar torn leather bracelet lay under one of the bookcases along the wall to her left. She hadn't noticed it the previous morning, although it did seem to lay undiscovered.

Was someone in my apartment? But I've just received access from the police. Has this been here the entire time? Maybe I haven't cleaned in a while.

Elizabeth reached into the side pocket of her trench coat and pulled out a pen. She scooped up the leather bracelet with the pen, careful not to touch it, and stood up. The apartment was silent. All she could hear was the ticking of the living room clock and the hum of the refrigerator at the front of her flat.

She pulled the bracelet towards her and breathed in its aroma. It smelt like a mixture of leather, musk, and a strange earthy scent that she couldn't put her finger on. But it was definitely a plant-based smell.

She gasped as a memory drifted into her mind.

———

A STIFF BREEZE drifted through the dig site. It was day three of the excavation, and Elizabeth was furious. After all the trouble of begging and reassuring investors and the NMA that archaeology's infamous looter, Maximilian Nicholls, was taking on an advisory role and would be no trouble, both he and Alistair were late. It was as if Alistair woke up one morning and decided what he really needed on the dig wasn't expertise or someone with connections, but instead a drinking buddy.

She felt like an idiot.

But she had one thing to be thankful for—nothing was missing and finding its way to the antiquities black market. To a certain extent, she held up her end of the bargain. He was, after all, no trouble.

Elizabeth took several deep breaths and pulled up the hood of her jacket. She clutched a cup of hot coffee and stared at the beautiful Cornwall sunrise. It was the start of a new day. Far off in the distance, a man walked towards the dig site. She crossed her arms. Elizabeth knew exactly who it was. As the anger built up inside, she reminded herself that murder was a crime, and she was too busy to serve a life sentence. She had too much work to do.

'Where have you been?' she yelled out at him.

'I guess that means you missed me.'

He smirked as he grabbed the cup from her hands. As he spun the mug around, a small piece of leather wrapped around his left wrist struck the side of the metal cup. He took a sip. 'That's awful.' He handed the cup to Elizabeth, turned around, and walked towards the dig site.

A DIGITAL *QUACK* shrilled out from her phone and jolted her back to reality. It was already half past nine. She was running out of time. As she replayed the moment in her mind, she doubted the integrity of the memory. She could have sworn that she saw Maximilian wearing the leather strap earlier that day when he waltzed into the dig site in the afternoon. But in her memory, she recalled seeing Alistair.

Maybe she wanted to believe that the man she'd married was completely innocent and not capable of murder or theft. That she hadn't spent five years dating, marrying, sleeping with, and eventually divorcing a criminal. It was entirely plausible that, if the bracelet belonged to Alistair, it might have been left after he checked out what she had done after their phone call earlier that morning. But she was torn between two possibilities. And she couldn't count on her recollection of events because it had been during the excavation of Excalibur that she started drinking again after a year of sobriety. Her memory was fractured.

Elizabeth slipped the leather strap into her pocket and made her way through her apartment. She was running out of time and grabbing breakfast and sprinting to the train station was more important. As she slammed the door behind her, she buttoned up her trench coat and tied the belt around her waist. She headed into the lift and struck the button for the ground floor.

A few minutes later, the doors sprang open, and she darted out of the elevator and towards the opened main gates.

Then it dawned on her. The leather strap was left after the police swept her apartment. Someone had returned to the crime scene.

Elizabeth looked down her street towards her apartment building. She froze as she felt a hand grip her shoulder and a gloved hand cover her mouth.

TWENTY

A SERIES of newspaper articles flashed across the screen as James perused the search results. Even with the introduction of modern technology, journalism was still in the Dark Ages. After all, journalism was an old man who moved slowly and often struggled to change. Many newspapers hadn't digitalised their archives, which meant individual journalists—or a dedicated research team—had to conduct research the old-fashioned way. So here he was, scrolling through articles stored on microfilm.

He paused and squinted at the screen. James rubbed the bridge of his nose as his glasses slid down his face. The yellow lights of the *British Library* newsroom were giving him a headache. This reading room was dedicated to news and was his favourite place to research. This afternoon, only a handful of people were clicking away at the mice on the other computers.

As his headache overpowered him, James refocused on the computer screen and scrolled to the next search result. It was another article about an archaeological discovery in Scotland with similar information as the previous article. Nothing new. Another article highlighted the turbulent nature of the archaeological world. There seemed to be an endless supply of examples of teams spending months away from home and then having an archaeological dig end up unsuccessful. He scrolled to the next article and sighed.

James picked up his smartphone and checked his email. There was nothing from Elizabeth. He scrolled through his emails, then looked up at the screen. It was odd. He had waited at the station for more than thirty minutes and missed his train, and she didn't pick up any of his calls. After all of that waiting, he boarded the next train to London. The most frustrating part was that he needed her help and expertise. Maybe it was a good thing she didn't turn up at the station. Anwar was quite clear on the conditions of her release, and leaving Northampton for London was one of them.

Could Elizabeth be afraid of Maximilian? Or maybe she's working with him?

He placed the phone on the desk and stared at the article in front of him. They might be working together to sell the sword to pay for their debts, and maybe Pippa had the same idea and got in the way. Perhaps this was why Elizabeth claimed to have slept through the events that occurred in her living room.

James narrowed his eyes on a single sentence in the middle of the screen. He smirked as he leaned back in his chair and stared at the image of Maximilian Nicholls being handcuffed on Christmas Day and dragged out of Alistair's family estate. James picked up his phone, selected Chan's number from a list of favourites, and listened to the dial tone.

'He was arrested for selling artefacts from an Egyptian tomb through Christie's in London,' James said the second the phone picked up.

'Who?' PC Chan asked as James hit the speaker icon.

'Maximilian Nicholls.' James had a slight smile on his face as he clicked through to the next article. 'I'm going to mention this in my daily report. Elizabeth thinks Maximilian is managing the business side of Alistair's business, and sourcing sponsors.'

'Really?' Chan's voice had a hint of curiosity.

'I think I'll need to look into the company's records, and maybe police records.'

'Of course you will,' Chan replied with a hint of sarcasm.

'I'm going to need some type of evidence to move forward. Just to check that I'm not going down the wrong path.' James stared at the image on the screen.

'Fine, you've piqued my interest. I'll apply for the warrants. And if I'm in a good mood, I'll let you know what I find,' Chan said as James hit the red button on the screen.

A rock formed at the pit of his stomach. All of this digging was not good for Valentine. But he was damned either way. Figuring out who was behind all of this would lead him to her. James couldn't sit still and wait, and he wasn't telling the police about her kidnapping.

I'm screwed. James sighed as he stared at the screen.

TWENTY-ONE

TUESDAY: 12:17 P.M.

MAXIMILIAN STARED at the screen and listened to the older man on the other end of the line go on and on about a series of worst-case scenarios. He leaned back in his chair in his first-floor office, looked out of the window and across the front lawn of the Carmichael Estate, and sighed.

He's going to pull out.

Maximilian continued to listen to the babble. This was the second investor in the last week. A drop of sweat dripped down his brow as he took a few deep breaths in an attempt to centre himself.

'I realise that it doesn't look great right now, but things are improving. The sword has been dated and valued. I assure you that you will receive a return on your investment.' Maximilian released his grip on the desk planner and rubbed the back of his neck. 'We have to be cautious and take all of the steps to authenticate the sword because there will be other experts who will do everything they can to discredit the find.'

'I understand that, but it's taking far too long,' the caller said.

'Elizabeth has been collecting data and preparing for

publication, a press launch, and securing a book deal,' Maximilian said as he tapped his index finger on the tabletop.

I'm kidding myself. There's no way we're going to get a book deal. And I've got bigger problems.

At first, this project had seemed exciting. Alistair had asked him to participate in the discovery of an infamous Arthurian artefact, and it all sounded so promising. Fourteen months had passed since that day, and now things were different. He was down two investors, possibly three, and spent his days lying to people about a return on investment.

'It's too risky. Did you hear me?' the man said with a hint of despair. 'It's been nine months since the discovery, and you have very little to show for it. Other than a valuation and confirmation of a period.'

'Just bear with us a little while longer.'

'No, I want my money back. I'm done.'

'We're so close. I swear I'll pay you out first before anyone else.'

'No, I want my money.'

'Either way, you need to give me a little time.'

'One week.' The man hung up.

———

MAXIMILIAN SLAMMED the phone down and stared at the spreadsheet on his screen. The truth was, no matter how much time this man gave him, he wasn't going to get his investment back. There was no money left to pay back the sponsors who were pulling out. Maximilian looked across the desk at the calendar, picked it up, and stared at the number on the page. He threw the calendar across the room and listened to it bounce off the wallpaper. His money problems had to wait because he had an even bigger problem.

Maximilian stared at the dial pad.

He said to never call.

Maximilian picked up the handset. He had reached a new level of desperation. As he dialled the number, he wondered what price he would pay for making this call. The line picked up.

'I know you said to never call you,' Maximilian started, tensely clutching the edge of his desktop planner. 'But we have a problem. A big problem. A journalist is sniffing around the sword. He's starting to—'

'I want his name,' said the voice at the other end of the line, talking over Maximilian.

'James Lalonde.'

'He's the chief editor of the *Northampton Tribune*. Are you sure?' the man with the New York accent said.

'You know of him?'

'Obviously.'

God, I'm in so much trouble.

Maximilian paused and took a deep breath through his nose.

How does a wealthy American collector in New York know about the editor of a tiny, insignificant newspaper in Northampton?

Maximilian tried to keep his composure as his eyes drifted to a framed photo of an elderly couple bearing the same bright blue eyes as his sitting on his desk. There was more at stake than a loss of funds and research being put on hold, especially for him.

'Yes, I'm sure. He turned up at Alistair's estate, and he knows about the sword.'

'Don't worry about him. If he's sniffing around, that means he doesn't have proof. No evidence. He's by the book. He will not print anything unless he has proof. It's now your job to make sure he doesn't find any.'

'You don't understand. He's so close to both of us.'

'You mean to you,' the voice on the line corrected him.

'How long do you think it will take him to connect all of this back to you?'

'You're being paranoid.'

'You're underestimating him.'

'He's playing mind games with you. He knows nothing.'

'One more thing,' Maximilian said into the telephone as his body stiffened. 'My parents?'

'They are well cared for.'

'It's been fourteen months.'

'Do what is required of you. And I will honour my end of the bargain,' the voice on the other end of the line said coldly.

Maximilian sighed and looked at the small clock on his desk.

'Let me make this simple for you,' the man said calmly. 'I want the sword. And it's become apparent to me that I need to step in and clean up after your mass incompetence.'

'Ah, sir. I can—' Maximilian heard an all too familiar click and a dial tone.

Shit. What have I done?

A bang echoed around the room as he slammed the handset down on his desk. He ran his fingers through his thick, dark hair and stared at the large red negative figures at the bottom of the spreadsheet on the screen.

TWENTY-TWO

TUESDAY: 3:48 P.M.

THE THICK WHIR of a machine frothing milk drowned out the voice at the end of the line. James placed his hand over his right ear as he pushed his phone closer towards his left ear. He grimaced.

'Yes, it's still his favourite coffeehouse. That man would take it intravenously if he could,' the voice on the other end of the line bellowed across the noise.

'Thanks. The last thing I want to do is upset him.'

He hit the red button on the screen and sighed. Lying was part of his job. He didn't like it, but no one liked talking to the press. Bending the truth had become a necessity. James had done his homework and discovered almost three hundred-plus scathing reviews of cafes all over Northampton by Pathologist Dr Olivier Deschamps. One rare favourable review indicated that he was a frequent patron of 'this establishment', as Olivier had worded it in a review on Google.

But James had been waiting for over two hours and saw no sign of the pathologist or his assistant. The man had a coffee problem, and he was nowhere in sight. Between line edits and proofs of the articles for the next day's edition and sips of coffee strong enough to cure heartburn, James had begun to get impatient. As he perused the article on his screen one last time, the front door to the cafe slammed open, breaking his concentration. James looked up, and across the room was a tall, thin man with salt-and-pepper hair. He wore a white lab coat from the Northampton General Hospital.

Jackpot.

James sprinted across the room, darting in and out of the sea of tables and chairs.

'Olivier,' he called out over the noise of the peak-hour trading.

Olivier waved at him, then returned his gaze to the menu.

'I heard you're performing the autopsy of Pippa Baker. She worked at the NMA with one of the curators, Elizabeth James. I'm doing a piece on Elizabeth's new exhibit for the culture section.'

Olivier raised his finger to silence James, leaned over the counter, and ordered his coffee.

He shook his head at James. 'You're starting with that? Here?' Olivier looked over the top of his thin-framed glasses.

'The other week at Queens Head, I listened to one of your exceptionally long monologues about how you despise all small talk and wish people would get straight to the point,' James said as he pointed towards the door, which was in the general direction of the pub.

'How do you know about the autopsy?'

'Anwar left his notes open on his desk.'

'He's getting sloppy in his old age.'

'Anwar is trying to—'

'I don't want to know.'

'This isn't a story for me. I'm looking into it for Elizabeth James. I believe she's innocent.'

'James, I don't want to know. I must remain objective.' Olivier clenched his right hand.

As Olivier turned around to walk out the door, James grabbed his bicep. 'Anwar is building a case against a suspect who I believe is innocent. Do you want her to go to jail for a crime she didn't commit?'

'That's not for me to decide. The evidence will speak for itself.'

'Just give me something. I need to know if my theory is correct, that I'm not wrong and helping a murderer go free.'

'No.' Olivier broke free from James's grip, marched to the door, and pulled it towards him.

'Obviously, this is completely off the record,' James said as Olivier paused, tapping his fingers on the doorframe.

The tall, lanky man walked towards James in complete silence. Olivier's light-brown eyes were cold and locked straight on him. Olivier stopped a few centimetres from where James was standing, then leaned in a little closer.

'I better not see a hint of this anywhere in your newspaper. I could get fired. The autopsy isn't finished yet.' Olivier's whisper was barely audible above the buzz of an overworked coffee machine at peak hour.

'Of course.'

'Whoever stabbed the deceased was taller, and I mean significantly taller.'

'Can you give me a figure?'

'It's just an estimate, but at least six feet, possibly taller.' Olivier walked out of the cafe then sprinted across the road towards the Northampton General Hospital.

———

A THICK STENCH of paper wafted past James's nose as he walked through the sea of cubicles and towards Chan's desk. The police constable whirled around on his chair and looked up at James, then focused back on the ever-growing sea of paperwork. James walked across the cubicle space as Chan stood and cleared away a pile of papers stacked up on the chair next to his desk. Chan paused for a moment. The PC's dark-brown eyes looked around his working area. Chan sighed, turned around, dumped the papers on the edge of his desk, and gestured to James to take a seat.

'I have the warrant. It came through an hour ago. While I was waiting for you, I got a little curious.' Chan sat down at his desk.

'And here I thought you were overworked and had no time.'

James walked to the desk, sat down, and leaned toward Chan. He rested his elbow on the corner of the desk.

'I have some time.' PC Chan shrugged.

'Just not for paperwork.' James smirked as his eyes lingered on the mounds of paper on Chan's desk.

'Your tips from the other day turned out to be quite helpful,' Chan said in a whisper.

James nodded. 'Out of curiosity, what was the murder weapon?'

Chan shook his head. 'A kitchen knife from Elizabeth's knife block. It's missing. This is feeding Anwar's suspicions surrounding Elizabeth's involvement in the murder. He thinks it was tossed in the garbage because the bins were emptied in her area the same morning that she called the police.'

James nodded.

'Off the record. Remember?' Chan pointed his finger at James.

'Yeah, yeah.'

'It was your daily report that sparked my interest. I looked up your friend Maximilian Arthur George Nicholls.' Chan raised his eyebrows at James. 'It's quite the name.'

'Let me guess? Old money.' James looked down at his dusty black shoes.

'Ancient.' Chan turned the screen towards James. 'But that's not as interesting as this.' Chan pointed at the screen.

James leaned in and squinted as his eyes swept the records. 'He's the CFO of Alistair's company?' James stared at Chan.

'Alistair is letting a man who was convicted of a felony run his company.'

'It wasn't a conviction. It was a slap on the wrist at best.' Chan shook his head.

'He was still convicted.' James tapped the pile of folders next to him.

'Yes. I'm going to take a stab in the dark and suggest that Alistair doesn't look at his company accounts,' PC Chan said as he raised his eyebrows.

'Possibly.'

'Trust me, he doesn't know a thing.' Chan reached across to the mouse and scrolled the small wheel while fixing his eyes on the screen.

James stood up, looked over Chan's shoulder, and read the data on the screen. 'That's a serious loss.' James paced.

After a few moments, he looked at Chan. 'How does Alistair not know? You would notice losing that much money.' James placed his hands on his hips, turned his head to the side, and stared straight ahead.

'You might. But Alistair comes from a very wealthy aristocratic family,' Chan said as James weighed up the new information.

'He must be in on this as well.' James took a deep breath and looked at his feet.

Chan rubbed the back of his neck, then closed the screen on his computer. 'I shouldn't be telling you this, but I found multiple texts between Pippa and Maximilian, and one where he explicitly told her to "keep out of it."'

James raised his eyebrows at Chan. 'Really? So, she must have interfered in something to do with the sword?'

Chan sighed.

'When I was in Pippa's flat, I noticed that she had a few expensive items that were probably gifts.' James nodded. 'And then there's the custom-made jacket that most likely belongs to Maximilian. Do you think they were in a romantic entanglement of some kind?'

Chan winced. 'Yes, there's evidence to suggest something was going on between them. I found chat messages and images on her computer when I returned to her flat in the Queens Head after that night. They were keeping it a secret.'

James groaned. 'So, why would he stab her if they're in a relationship? Did she just get in the way?' James nodded. 'It fits with his icy manner, I suppose.'

Chan grabbed the mouse and opened a screen on his computer. 'I can't continue speculating with you. It's unprofessional. But if there's anything else you know, you should tell me now.'

James took a deep breath and remained silent.

Chan turned around, looked up at James, and tilted his head.

'Nope,' James said with a nod.

'There's one more thing I need to show you,' Chan said as James looked up and focused on the screen.

'What?' James's voice had a hint of curiosity.

'Maximilian has accumulated a significant debt since his conviction and fine.'

James walked across the room towards Chan's desk and looked at the report on the screen. His heart sank.

What have I gotten myself into?

James clutched the middle button that closed his suit jacket and paced the room again.

I'm sorry, Valentine.

James stopped in the centre of the room and sighed. Things were hopeless, but he couldn't give in to his pessimistic nature. He had to keep going, piecing together the clues, one by one.

The note bore a set of explicit instructions. But that was all he could think about—Valentine. He needed to focus on the case and close in on Maximilian and Alistair. But he couldn't get her out of his mind. The more he pushed the thoughts away, the more they resurfaced.

A tingling sensation built up in James's chest as he swallowed a hard lump in his throat. There was a part of him that desperately wanted a second chance to make things right. But he knew Valentine and sensed that she would not give him the opportunity.

'What's wrong?' Chan stood up from his chair, walked over to James, and placed his hand on his back.

James took a deep breath to centre himself, then turned to Chan.

'They have Valentine,' he whimpered as he blinked away the tears. 'I'm certain.'

TWENTY-THREE

TUESDAY: 4:45 P.M.

THE DOOR FLEW OPEN, and a loud bang filled the room as it struck the wall on the other side. Alistair shot through the doorframe and dived in and out through the sea of workstations towards Chan.

'Hey,' a junior constable cried out as he chased the lanky man.

James tensed and sucked up his tears before he glared at Alistair, who stopped a few inches from where they were standing.

As Alistair opened his mouth, he paused for a moment. He appeared to reconsider his actions, but it was too late. James could feel Alistair's gaze lingering on his watering eyes.

'I'm sorry.' Alistair bowed his head and took a few steps back.

A junior officer appeared behind Alistair, grabbed his right bicep, and squeezed it tight.

'Sorry, Chan. He followed someone through the doors at reception,' the red-faced junior constable said as he tried to drag Alistair away from Chan's workstation.

'She's missing,' Alistair said as he inched forward and pulled a note and picture from his tweed-checked jacket.

'Get me some gloves.' Chan looked over Alistair's shoulder at the younger constable. 'Is your note similar to this one?' Chan refocused on James.

'Yes, I found it pinned to my refrigerator with a kitchen knife along with a photo,' James said as his eyes glazed over.

'I want to see both of your items.'

'I was told not to go to the police.' James faced Chan.

'We will find them both,' Chan said as he studied the note in Alistair's hand.

James glanced at Alistair. 'How do we know that you're not behind all of this?'

'I beg your pardon.' Alistair adjusted his bow tie.

'You heard me.'

Alistair glared at James and stepped back into the passageway between the workstations.

'I still love Elizabeth,' Alistair said. 'She drives me insane, but every time I see her—' He took a deep breath. 'I still want to be with her again. We allowed work to get in the way of our relationship. We spent so much time in the field—discovering, studying, and researching—that we neglected the most important thing we had, which was us.'

'Anyone can say they love someone. That doesn't mean you didn't do this. How do I know you haven't done something unspeakable to get Elizabeth to take you back?' James faced Alistair and observed his reaction.

'This isn't some elaborate scheme so I can turn up and play the part of the brave knight rescuing a damsel in distress.' Alistair glared at James.

That sounded a little too rehearsed.

James raised his eyebrows at Alistair.

'If you must know the ins and outs of my relationship, then you might find it interesting that I shared a moment of passion with Elizabeth during her recent dig.'

James sighed. He was caught in an awkward place where he had to trust a potential suspect based on his word and his word alone. There was no way Alistair could prove his innocence or the claims he was making. After all, his claims were based on emotion.

The junior officer returned to Chan's workstation and held up a pair of gloves wrapped in plastic. As Chan grabbed the gloves, Alistair softened his gaze towards James.

'Valentine is missing as well. And presumably kidnapped by the same person as Elizabeth.' Alistair stepped into James's personal space. 'That's why you're so interested in my career, business, and Maximilian. You believe we have Valentine. And you're just hanging around to collect the evidence.'

'If you love Elizabeth as much as you claim, then you must understand my actions. After all, isn't there a part of you that wants to tear this city apart until you find her?'

Chan sighed and, with his gloved hand, grabbed the ivory sheet of paper and placed it in a clear evidence bag.

'What is it?' James asked.

'I doubt we'll find any evidence on this.' Chan studied the contents of the evidence bag.

'Very well. If you insist on turning the city upside down, then I'll join you.' Alistair offered his hand to James.

'I have to go back to the office for a few hours, then I'm free to meet up with you. And before I leave, there's something you should know.'

'There's more?' Alistair was wide-eyed.

'Yes, but I need to put the morning's edition of the *Tribune* to bed. I've got hours of work ahead of me.' James ran his fingers through his thick, dark blond hair.

Alistair nodded. 'I can wait. I've got nothing but time.'

With a nod towards the exit, James and Alistair sauntered through the sea of cubicles as James shared his latest findings. Shock swept across Alistair's face as he heard the news about his financial records.

How can he be in the dark about his own company's finances?

TWENTY-FOUR

TUESDAY: 5:15 P.M.

A FAMILIAR SCENT of dust and clay floated by her nose as she slowly opened her eyes. She closed them again as a sharp pain shot across her forehead. Elizabeth opened her eyes a second time. Off in the distance stood a tall, familiar figure.

Unbelievable.

She narrowed her eyes to sharpen her blurry vision.

It wasn't the situation she found herself in that was unbelievable; it was more the lengths this man had gone to, all for the sake of cash flow. Then again, part of her wasn't surprised at all. Elizabeth had known involving him would come back to bite her, but she'd never expected it to happen this quickly or for the cost to be this high.

As her vision cleared, Maximilian's piercing blue eyes and chiselled jawline came into view. She didn't understand how someone so attractive could be so dark and cruel. The tall, dark-haired man lifted his muscular frame off the table and walked towards her. As he approached, she saw the desperation in his eyes.

The remaining pieces of the sword are safe for now.

She kept her eyes on him as he stopped and towered over her. He reached out and lowered her gag.

'You do realise that I know where I am?' Elizabeth looked at the dusty shelves.

Maximilian shrugged.

Elizabeth looked back at him. 'I can't believe you killed Pippa.'

'Based on the fact that I haven't been pulled in for questioning, I can assume that all you have is a conspiracy theory and no actual facts.' Maximilian scratched his temple.

Elizabeth narrowed her eyes. 'So, you're playing innocent.'

'He has my parents and has injected my mother with some kind of virus—I don't quite understand how it all works. But, I'm at his mercy. The deal is I do exactly what he says. And in return, my mother will be put on a drug that his company is trialling and live.' A pinched expression swept across his face.

Elizabeth struggled against her bonds. 'You're an idiot if you think this will turn out well for you.'

Closing his eyes, Maximilian took a deep breath, then opened them again slowly. 'You're asking me to choose between my mother and saving your career from your own stupid mistakes?'

'I guess we both know how quickly you can make that decision.' Elizabeth cocked her head to the side and raised her eyebrows.

Maximilian shrugged. 'You seem so sure about everything, don't you?'

Elizabeth leaned back in the chair and looked up at the man towering over her. 'I told you at the Victoria and Albert Museum event that he would be trouble, but you wouldn't listen.'

Maximilian shook his head. 'You had no money to fund the dig other than the little money the council gave you. I did what was necessary.'

'I never asked you to rush in and save the day.'

'Where's the rest of the sword?' Maximilian walked towards the desk, sat down, and crossed his arms.

'I don't know what you mean,' she said as she struggled against her bonds one more time.

'The sword is in pieces. We're both aware of this. I was there for the discovery.'

'Have you stopped to consider why he wants the sword and what he might do with it?' Elizabeth said, softening her tone.

'One problem at a time.' Maximilian rubbed his hand over the top of the desk as if he were in deep thought.

'I will not let you hand over the sword to him. Not after everything I've been through to get it. And I have my reputation to think of,' Elizabeth said as she glanced over at the rows of shelves.

Maximilian stood up and walked towards Elizabeth. He bent down, gripped the back of her chair, and raised his eyebrows at her. 'I think your professional reputation will survive this. You have a life raft hovering around you with connections, eager to save the day.'

As Maximilian stared at her, faint screams cried out, far off in the distance.

'What have you done?' Elizabeth looked towards the shelves, knowing that in one of the other archives, in the basement of the Northampton Museum of Anthropology, another woman was in trouble.

'Where is it?' He inched closer to her.

She could feel his grip tighten on the chair. 'You've made a mistake.' Elizabeth looked into his eyes. *Keep it together. I don't want this jerk to have the satisfaction of knowing I'm terrified.*

'Where's the rest of the sword?' He shook her chair violently, and the room spun.

'It was all in my office before I left for the dinner in London. I swear, it was there. Perhaps someone else beat you to it.'

'Do you expect me to believe your bullshit story?'

Maximilian stood up and placed his hands on his hips. 'I've checked the museum database, and it shows that you recorded one piece of the sword.'

'If you say so.' Elizabeth shrugged.

'You've purposely hidden the remaining pieces.'

'I listed the sword as one item. There's no need to register the individual pieces. Don't tell me how to do my job.'

Elizabeth tried to lean forward against her bonds.

'I'm done playing nice with you.' Maximilian picked up a pair of pliers off the dusty metal shelves behind him.

Another muffled scream echoed across the archives.

'Who is the other woman you have locked down here?'

'Why are you so concerned about some random scream? You have far bigger problems.' Her captor inched toward her, opened the pliers, then fixed his gaze on her bound hands.

TWENTY-FIVE

TUESDAY: 5:44 P.M.

JAMES THREW his suit jacket over the back of his chair and sighed. Although he had accomplished a substantial amount of work, he was still behind. James rubbed his eyes, pulled the chair out, and sat at his desk. As he looked at the light flashing on his phone, a familiar-looking piece of ivory paper caught his attention from the floor in his doorway. His body tensed and his eyes widened. A pain shot across his chest as he continued to stare at the page.

How did he deliver it and go unnoticed? The letter wasn't there a moment ago.

James continued to stare at the lone piece of paper. He didn't want to walk across the room and pick up the sheet. Not that he had to—he knew what it contained. All roads had led to this point. It was inevitable. What was unclear was how much research Maximilian had done on him.

As James leaned on his desk and stood, it occurred to him.

Does Maximilian have a contact at the paper?

He grabbed a tissue off his desk, sauntered towards the ivory page, and squatted down. His hands trembled as he flipped the piece of paper over.

It was just as he'd expected. Cut-out letters arranged across the page revealed a message. A predictable message. But this time, it had one extra feature.

I've got you.

James smiled as he walked to his phone, tapped the screen several times, and waited for the dial tone. 'He's delivered the ransom note,' James said the second the call connected.

'Why are you so happy?' Chan had a hint of suspicion in his voice.

'It contains a bonus.'

'What bonus?'

'He's fucked up. There's a smudged partial print at the top left-hand corner of the page.' James stared at the blood.

I hope this doesn't belong to Valentine.

James continued to stare at the note.

'What does it say? How much does he want?'

'Don't worry about it. I can pay the ransom.'

James fixed his eyes on the scrapbook-style letters.

'How much?' Chan raised his voice.

'One hundred and fifty thousand pounds in twenty-pound notes in nonsequential order. I'm to show up and drop off the money at a warehouse along Alexander Avenue, and then he will drop Valentine off at my house a few hours later,' James said.

'You're insane if you go along with this. You know how this will end.' Chan's sigh rang through the tiny speaker.

'He needs the money. He'll follow through with the deal.'

'How are you going to get that much money?' Chan asked.

'I've got it under control.' James hung up.

So, he's done a background check.

He was so desperate to get Valentine back he hadn't considered the obvious outcome, the terrible way a lot of kidnappings ended. Was Chan right? Was he a fool for thinking he could get her back?

TWENTY-SIX

WEDNESDAY: 1:12 A.M.

ALISTAIR RUBBED the back of his neck as he stood next to the round table in the centre of the foyer. His hair looked as if he had brushed it back multiple times. Alistair's hands trembled, and his eyes looked wild. Perhaps James had misjudged him. Maybe his feelings and concern were genuine. He wanted to believe this, no matter how naïve it sounded. Journalism had created a cynicism that ran deep within his veins.

As he stepped into the foyer, James's eyes spotted scattered archive boxes. Newspapers were strung across the round table in the centre, where a large arrangement of flowers had stood a few days earlier. It was as he had expected. What lay before him was the result of a desperate man with time on his hands.

Since 5:45 in the evening, James had received an hourly phone call from Alistair, alerting him to a whole range of situations. Every call ended the same way and with the same question: what time do you want to meet up?

After a series of meetings, edits, and the final approvals of the layout, he was done. All James wanted to do was sleep, but Alistair was having none of that. James gave in to Alistair's demands. Here he was, at 1:12 a.m. the next morning, babysitting a distraught aristocrat.

'I couldn't find Maximilian anywhere, and I've called everyone I know, and no one has seen Elizabeth—no one. I've searched her house, spoken to her neighbours. No one saw anything.' Alistair paced the width of the foyer.

Excellent. I'm giving up sleep for a recap of the last eight hours.

Alistair stopped, struck the pile of archive boxes in front of him, and sighed.

'I've even gone through my company's records out of desperation, hoping to find a warehouse or rental receipt, although I haven't checked Maximilian's family properties.' Alistair faced James.

'He will not keep Valentine and Elizabeth at a location that'll be traced back to him.' James walked over to the archive boxes and placed a hand on Alistair's shoulder. 'The only way we'll find the girls is if he made an significant mistake. It's how most people are caught. And that's what we'll do.'

'But I've searched everything,' Alistair said in a distraught tone as he hunched over the archive boxes and rested his head in his hands.

'Where is your office? Is it close by?'

Alistair pointed towards the staircase. 'Upstairs. I've checked it.'

———

JAMES ASCENDED the central staircase to the next level. He floated his left hand along the polished wooden bannister as he dragged his weary feet up the plush carpeted steps. As James approached the top, he saw the first door ajar, revealing a sea of paperwork.

Three guesses as to what happened in here.

He walked across the landing and pushed the door. As it

crept open, he scanned the mess that lay before him. James turned around to find Alistair standing behind him.

'I'm assuming you did this?'

Alistair shrugged. 'Of course.'

'You realise you've touched everything in this room and may have potentially contaminated any evidence?' James looked at him. 'I know how you feel and that you're just trying to find something that will point you towards Elizabeth's whereabouts, but you know PC Chan may look at this in a suspicious light.'

Alistair placed his hands on his hips. 'I've done nothing wrong. I checked up on Elizabeth to find her missing. And then I found the note.'

James sighed and viewed the sea of paperwork strung across the floor.

Did he have to tear the room apart like a madman?

He looked at Alistair. 'If the unspeakable happens and we never see the girls again, whether ransoms are paid or not, if we find anything in this room that links any of these events with Maximilian, it may not stand up in a court of law. And may be dismissed from a trial.'

'There's no need for the dramatics,' Alistair said.

James walked across the room, stepping on the bare patches of carpet but avoiding the mess. He pulled out a pair of white gloves that were folded in a small zip-lock bag and put them on, then he tucked the small bag into his jacket.

'What do you want me to do?' Alistair asked, interrupting James's concentration.

James nearly ran his fingers through his hair in frustration, catching himself and dropping his hands back to his sides only when he saw the gloves on his hands and reminded himself that they were for more than fingerprints. He turned to the anxious aristocrat. 'Ideally, touch nothing but, if you insist on helping, you must find a pair of gloves. Just in case you can't resist.' James whirled around and continued to tiptoe around the room, not knowing where to start.

'Very well.' Alistair headed towards the door.

'Is Maximilian the only person who works in this room?'

'Yes, I have a separate study down the hall.'

'What's in the room next door?' James pointed towards the wall on the other side of the antique desk.

'That was Elizabeth's office. I haven't touched it since she left.' Alistair slipped his hands in his pockets and looked at the ground. 'I guess you could say that I'm a hopeless romantic.'

Alistair turned and continued his trek towards the ground level, disappearing out of sight.

James stood in the centre of the office and surveyed the room. He realised that the most logical place to search was the large antique mahogany desk.

He walked around the desk and ran his fingers along the large leather chair. James looked down and saw an immaculately folded grey cable-knit sweater on the chair. He reached out and pulled the crewneck down to reveal the letters "XXL" on the tag.

Bingo.

The desktop was neat, almost pristine. A small frame containing a photo of an elderly couple sat untouched on the far right-hand side of the desk.

Perhaps this was the original state of the office before Alistair came tearing through it like a bull in a China shop.

James lowered himself onto the chair. At first glance, Maximilian had seemed meticulous, so the likelihood of finding a trail of evidence was zero. However, James wasn't ready to give up. All he wanted was a small clue.

Apart from an archive box discarded in the middle of the desk where a computer screen had once lay, the desk was minimalistic in terms of decoration. James ran his fingers along the leather mat at the centre of the desk and down the side of a small set of drawers underneath the tabletop. He pulled at the little handle.

'I look like a creepy street magician,' Alistair said as he burst through the door, holding his white-gloved hands in front of him.

Still clutching the handle of the drawer, James pulled, but it wouldn't budge. He ran his fingers under the desk and discovered a concealed wooden tray. He pulled it towards himself. A small, rusted key lay face up on the shelf. James narrowed his eyes as he stared at the antique. Something was not right about this; it seemed too easy.

Why would someone with great attention to detail leave a key like this lying around?

James picked up the key, inserted it into the lock, and turned it. After a small click sounded, the drawer released. Inside the first drawer lay a Japanese puzzle box. James lifted it out and shook it. To his surprise, the clinking of metal sliding across a wooden interior called out from within.

The contents of the puzzle box clanged in protest as James continued to violently shake the wooden box close to his ear. He arose from the desk, clutching the box, and started sliding the pieces. He listened to the corresponding clicks as he began to circle the room.

————

AFTER THIRTY MINUTES of pacing and listening to Alistair's endless babble, James was verging on losing it.

'You'll never open that,' Alistair said, as he followed James around the room. 'Maximilian is obsessed with Japanese culture and those thingamabobs.' Alistair waved his index finger at the box in James's hand.

James rolled his eyes at the voice of doom standing in front of him and shifted around to the window. The pressure from his small audience of one was getting to him. He needed to concentrate. He had one final move left before he had to reset the puzzle box.

As James listened to the dull click created by turning the box's last element, the lid popped open. He held his breath as he looked down. After multiple combinations and resets, it was open. But he hadn't considered what lay inside. It might be a valuable personal keepsake and not at all related to the last forty-eight hours. At this point, he didn't care. James slid the top of the box open, and his heart sank as he looked inside.

A bright rose-gold watch with the words Ted Baker engraved on the clock face lay inside, along with a gold chain bearing a heart-shaped locket no bigger than his thumb. James pulled out the tiny pendant and placed the puzzle box on the filing cabinet that rested under the large window. He stared at the locket, then flipped it over. Etched into the gold-plated metal were two small letters, "E" and "C."

Just two simple letters. They said so little, but so much at the same time.

I should've insisted on staying with Elizabeth for the rest of the morning.

James flipped the locket over. A small click filled the quiet room as he opened it. Inside, a picture of a younger Alistair stared back at him.

His story about pining after his lost love has checked out.

James spun around to find Alistair standing in the middle of the room, watching him. James observed Alistair for a few more moments. It was as if he was holding his breath in anticipation.

'It looks like you're not the only one that's harbouring feelings.' James flattened his hand to reveal the open locket.

Alistair lunged forward and stared at the small piece of metal cradled in James's gloved hand.

'Don't touch it.' James pulled the locket closer towards him. He sighed and placed the locket back in the puzzle box.

'Valentine's watch is in here too. I don't understand why

Maximilian would keep these items in his office.' James pulled out a zip-lock bag from inside his grey suit jacket and opened it.

'Maybe it's proof he has the girls, in case we didn't believe him,' Alistair said with a shrug. He approached the filing cabinet, then leaned over and looked into the box. 'Good job opening the box. You're almost like a modern-day Poirot.'

'He's Belgian,' James mumbled faintly.

'He's almost French.'

James shook his head as he picked up the puzzle box, then placed it in the bag and sealed it.

'You look so depressed. You should be happy. We're one step closer to finding the girls. And possibly a reconciliation.' Alistair patted James on the back.

'For you, maybe.' James pulled out his smartphone and tapped at the screen. *Valentine is never going to take me back.*

'Oh, come on. Stop being so pessimistic.'

'Valentine has made up her mind. There's nothing I can do to change it. I fear it's much too late to save our relationship.' James's eyes glazed over.

'Things aren't all rosy for me either. My business is in financial trouble, and I was in the dark the entire time.' Alistair placed his hands in his pockets, then looked at the floor.

'Why did you put a man with a criminal record in charge of the finances of your business?'

'You don't waste any time, do you?'

'I find it strange that you wouldn't keep tabs on a man like that.'

'Maximilian is a dear friend. I went to university with his younger brother. His not-so-great decisions result from pressure from his father to excel and further the family name, so to speak. It's something I can relate to.'

'So, you made a business decision from a place of sentiment?'

'No, it was more than that. Maximilian has charm and business sense and archaeological experience. Well, he had business sense. At least I thought he did,' Alistair said, as if reading James's mind.

'And you have experience and knowledge about the Arthurian legend and its grounding in reality.'

'Exactly. We both bring something to the table.'

'The kidnappings make little sense. If Maximilian has the sword, then why hasn't he sold it? Wouldn't that fix the cash flow issues?'

'It's a little more complicated than that, but the investors are expecting a return on investment. They're also expecting to see publications and newspaper articles and progress reports. None of this is possible if the sword remains missing and isn't returned to the NMA.' Alistair stared at the desk and pursed his lips.

'But why would he need more money? Isn't the sword valued at five million pounds?'

'That's just an estimate. The sword wouldn't be as easy to sell as you might think. We found the sword in pieces. It took months to find the last piece.' Alistair paced the room. 'Because of its delicate parts, the number of interested buyers would be limited. And that's not ideal.'

'He doesn't have all the pieces.' James whirled around and pointed at Alistair.

Alistair's eyes bulged. 'You're a genius.'

TWENTY-SEVEN

WEDNESDAY: 2:42 A.M.

IT HAD TAKEN James almost ninety minutes to go through every item in Maximilian's office before he realised his search was fruitless. All he had were two items that linked Maximilian to the missing women. Nothing else. Not a single ounce of evidence pointed towards the location where he could find Valentine and Elizabeth. Upon admitting defeat, Alistair talked James into coming down to the library and having a drink to mull the situation over.

It was 2:24 a.m., and James collapsed in an armchair, his suit jacket lying across the three-seater sofa in front of him. He sighed as he clutched the glass of rum. Taking a sip, he grimaced as the alcohol burned the back of his throat. Alistair sat in the armchair next to James and grabbed a glass from a small, round table. A faint smell of polish lingered in the air. James watched as Alistair, sitting cross-legged in the chair next to him, surveyed the tall mahogany bookshelves.

For someone with a missing loved one, he seems tranquil.

James pulled the glass from his lips and rested it on the arm of his chair. He stared into the brownish liquid and calculated his next move. James took a deep breath as he turned his head towards Alistair. Even though James was weary, he didn't have the luxury of resting. He had to get back to work.

'So, we can assume that Maximilian kidnapped Elizabeth for two reasons. The first, she got too close or knew too much. And when I showed up and questioned her, Maximilian kidnapped Elizabeth to keep her from saying something,' James recounted, waving his glass in the air.

'And the second reason?' Alistair placed his glass on the table.

'He knew the sword came in pieces and couldn't get the information anywhere else.' James put his glass down and dabbed a spill on his tie with the napkin that had been resting on the other arm of the chair. 'I'm expecting to find her office at the NMA ransacked, and maybe her home office.'

'That doesn't explain why he has Valentine.' Alistair had a sympathetic look in his eye.

'I got too close, and he needs the money. Perhaps one of your investors is squeezing him for ROI.'

'Sounds about right,' Alistair said after a few moments. 'Most people are impatient and expect quick results.' He stared straight ahead.

'What if we go back to her offices and retrace her steps?' James placed the napkin on the table and inspected the damage on his tie from the spill.

'Why?' Alistair screwed up his face.

'Well, we could figure out where she's hiding the pieces and locate them before Maximilian figures it out. We could trade the pieces for Elizabeth and Valentine,' James said as Alistair picked up his glass and took another sip.

'Elizabeth has probably told him where the pieces are by now.'

'No—' James picked up the glass from the table next to him, '—she's far too stubborn for that. I don't see her giving out that information too soon.'

'I guess.' Alistair finished his drink. 'You don't think he will hurt her?'

'No,' James lied. 'But we're short on time.'

THREE PAINTINGS of French chateaux hung on the walls in Elizabeth's office. James stared into his barely recognisable reflection in the glass. Long gone were the days where he could pull an all-nighter and still look fresh as a daisy the next morning. He sighed as he placed the final stack of paperwork on the white desk in the centre of the office.

Journals and PhD theses, all bearing sticky notes with illegible scribbles, filled her tiny office. Elizabeth showed no signs of slowing down. She had an addiction. He looked up at the empty glass case. The white bookshelves were covered with black fingerprint powder.

Why did she take the sword home with her? Did she suspect Maximilian would try to steal it? And if so, why did she make it easy for him?

'This stuff is everywhere.' Alistair ran his finger along the glass case, disturbing the fresh coating of white dust.

'I don't know what I was hoping to find, but it wasn't mountains of paperwork,' James said as he ran his fingers through the pile of papers he had just skimmed through.

'I need coffee.' Alistair pulled out another set of journals from the shelves.

'Perfect. You get the coffee while I continue searching the rest of the apartment.' James walked out of the office, then down the hall and towards the main bedroom.

————

TWENTY MINUTES LATER, James was sitting at the edge of Elizabeth's bed, flipping through the third travel guide he'd found in the top drawer of her bedside table. One guidebook, he could understand, but three was obsessive. Each guide rehashed the same information and missed out on the most beautiful parts of France, areas off the well-worn tourist trail. They were places his grandparents had dragged him to when he was younger. His summers comprised visits to an endless number of chateaux with rare book collections and abbeys. It was as if his grandfather wanted to visit them all before he died. In those libraries, James developed a love of literature.

James closed the book and sighed. He missed his grandparents. It was becoming unbearable to flip through the pages of the book without reliving those moments.

Elizabeth shared his grandfather's love of mediaeval chateaux, as evidenced by the sticky tabs placed throughout the pages of all three books. As he threw the third travel guide into the bedside table, a Eurostar Standard Premier boarding pass to Paris floated out from the pages and onto the floor. The date on the ticket was the eighth of July, eight days after the end of the dig. James crouched down and slipped the ticket into the inner pocket of his jacket. Then he pulled the three travel guides out of the bedside table drawer for a second time.

A bang echoed through the apartment.

'Sorry it took so long. The service was a nightmare,' a voice called out from the front of the apartment. 'I had to order three times.'

James looked down at the travel guides and wondered if he

should tell Alistair about the ticket or keep it to himself. As James pondered the root of his newfound paranoia, Alistair barged in through the door while holding two cups of coffee and a brown paper bag. A buttery aroma filled the tiny bedroom and enticed James to smile at Alistair.

'Some light reading?'

'Maybe these could hold a few answers.' James followed Alistair out of the bedroom and towards the living room. 'I realise that I'm probably reaching, but it could lead us somewhere.'

———

IT WAS as James had expected. Someone had been through Elizabeth's office at the NMA before him. Papers were scattered across the desktop and across the floor. Filing cabinets were left hanging open. And based on the carnage that surrounded him, their search was fruitless. He was tempted to point the blame at Maximilian, but it all seemed too easy. Almost too convenient. Or maybe Anwar was right —he had a gap in the front page to fill and missed the excitement that came with chasing a story. For now, James was sticking with "too convenient".

James stood at the door and took in the scene. His eyes wandered through the trail of shattered ceramic treasures on the floor to find a way through the mess without disturbing the evidence. Alistair pushed past him and meandered around the office. It wasn't the aimlessness of a first-time visitor. His route seemed purposeful, like he had been there before.

Alistair leaned over and rummaged through the open drawer.

'Be careful of the broken pottery pieces,' James said as Alistair looked up at him.

'They're forgeries.' Alistair continued to rummage through the drawer.

James rolled his eyes as he tiptoed into the office and stopped in front of the bookshelf behind the seat where he had been only a few days earlier. He pulled out the books, checking to see if anything lay hidden behind or between the pages.

James froze.

He stared at the last book on the shelf. It seemed so out of place. The book was a limited edition of *Pride and Prejudice* by Jane Austen. He pulled the cloth-covered hardback from the shelf. James ran his fingers along the thick pages in an attempt to pry them apart, but they were stuck together. As he flipped the cover open, he found the book was hollow, and it contained a collection of receipts.

'I didn't have you pegged as an Austen fan,' Alistair said from the corner of Elizabeth's office.

'It's full of receipts.' James looked back at him. 'It's unorganised. I can't figure out if it's all work or personal expenses.'

He pulled out a paper receipt from The Olive Garden in Tintagel.

'That must be from the dig.' Alistair dismissed the receipt, pulled it out of James's hand, and threw it back inside the book.

James picked up the receipt and stared at the date on the bottom. 'No, the date is wrong. It's more recent than that.' James continued to stare at the receipt. 'Was the sword excavated nearby?'

'It's a long shot,' Alistair said. 'Maybe she hid a piece of the sword there, but it seems too obvious.'

'I'll see if I can get someone from IT to grant me access to her computer to check for any appointments. I'd imagine she couldn't have visited the site without an official appointment.' James pulled out his phone and tapped on the screen.

Alistair picked up the Olive Garden receipt and studied it. 'No, the castle ruins are back open for tourists. She wouldn't need an appointment. I'd imagine she showed up, hid the piece, and left.'

———

FIFTEEN MINUTES LATER, James found a vehicle hire receipt from a company in Paris, a receipt from a local brasserie in the city of Pierrefonds, and a speeding ticket from the French police that she'd received somewhere along the D973. He smiled to himself. All these events had taken place within the same time frame; on the same day as the Eurostar ticket.

'The quickest way to travel to the castle ruins in Tintagel is by car,' Alistair said. 'I'll go because I'm familiar with the Arthurian legend. I've worked at the site, and I know my way around. If it happens to be closed, I'll get better access.'

'Sounds good.' James nodded. 'I've found a receipt to a bakery in France that's within walking distance of a chateau in Pierrefonds. It could be a long shot, but I think she may have hidden a piece there. My grandfather is a chateau enthusiast like your lady. I think he'll be able to get me into a few of the more restricted sections of the chateau.'

'Yes, I think we've spent far too long here already. We should move along and travel to our respective destinations. I think it's better if we get to the pieces before anyone else while we have the advantage.' Alistair grabbed the hollowed-out book from James's hand and placed it back on the shelves.

Amongst the receipts, James felt the coolness of a piece of metal. He looked at the receipts and moved them around in his hand as Alistair guided him towards the door.

'James, we need to leave. I'm worried that Maximilian might come back. And if he does, we're both screwed.' Alistair closed the oak door to Elizabeth's office behind them.

James stared at the rusted metal in his hand and slipped it into his pocket. Alistair grimaced at the letters etched into the gold plate on the door. There was something odd about the way Alistair was pushing him away from Elizabeth's office. Alistair was playing the part of the estranged, stressed-out lover too well. It was almost as if Alistair was trying to distract him from a trail of clues James hadn't found earlier. Or maybe he was blaming Alistair because he had sat face to face with the man who kidnapped Valentine a few days earlier and didn't see the clues. Perhaps it was easier to believe the man in front of him was playing a role instead of suffering at the hand of his poor judgement.

'She changed her name.' Alistair pointed towards the name etched into the gold plate. 'She's dropped my last name.'

'I'm sorry.' James placed his hand on Alistair's shoulder.

Alistair stared at the name plaque on the closed door. 'It's been changed, and so soon.'

James grabbed Alistair by the arm. 'We should leave. At this point, you're just torturing yourself.'

The two men strolled away from Elizabeth's office and through the museum towards the street parking. Still clutching the receipts and the secret fragment of the sword, James said goodbye to Alistair and planned an impromptu trip to France in his mind as he dashed towards his red Peugeot.

TWENTY-NINE

TINTAGEL CASTLE, CORNWALL U.K.

ALISTAIR PULLED up the collar of his dark-grey jacket as the chill in the air blew straight through his body. It was three-thirty in the afternoon, in May, and the cool breeze from the shoreline made the temperature feel as if it had dropped below ten degrees. Finding the missing pieces of the sword proved to be harder than he had first expected. He was sure he knew where Elizabeth had hid a piece here. Two hours had passed since he first arrived, and he was empty-handed.

He paused, leaned against the narrow-arched doorway, and looked out at the blue-green ocean crashing into the rocks below. The stone staircase ran down to the shoreline along one of the few intact walls at Tintagel.

Where did you hide it, Lizzie?

Alistair turned around in the doorway, looked across at the stone ruins, and sighed.

It had been over fourteen months since he and Elizabeth had sat on the stone stairs, looked out at the ocean, and kissed. The first time in two years. Things were different; he could feel her drifting away. And he wondered if she would ever take him back after the events that had unfolded over the last few days. But there was no use in crying over that now.

As he stepped out of the doorway, onto the stone floor of the castle, his hand brushed along the wooden door. The wood felt smoother than when he was last here. Alistair turned around one last time to take in the view of the shoreline. Out of the corner of his eye, he caught a shimmer of what he hoped was metal coming from within the jagged stone wall. It was most likely a piece of rubbish stuffed into the holes by a tourist.

Some people have no respect.

Alistair stepped closer to the small hole in the wall. He smiled as he inserted his first two fingers into the stone pocket. His fingers grazed a familiar, rough piece of metal.

She was feeling sentimental, after all.

Alistair pulled out the piece of metal and cradled it in his hands. Elizabeth had taken a significant risk by hiding the parts in such a public place. It was almost a miracle that someone had not found it first.

He pulled a white cloth from the left pocket of his jacket, folded it up with the piece of metal inside, then tucked it back into his pocket. Out of his right pocket, Alistair pulled out a smartphone and typed the message:

> Found it. Two more pieces to go!

He hesitated and stared at the screen as he waited for the message to go through. A short chime broke the silence of the castle ruins. The message had been sent. There was no going back. Alistair tapped the screen again and composed another new message:

> James, someone else is looking for the pieces and got to the ruins before me. Be careful!

THIRTY

PIERREFONDS, FRANCE

'TOO SLOW.' Dr Francois Lalonde slapped the steering wheel of his mustard-coloured Renault.

How do you not have severe blood pressure problems?

James laughed to himself as his grandfather screamed at the cautious driver in front. He looked out the window from the road leading to the majestic Chateau de Pierrefonds. A dense green forest surrounded the castle walls. All he could see was the tops of the castle and the four protective towers—a beautiful sight.

'*Papi.*' James faced his grandfather and braced himself for the inevitable fallout. 'You can't come with me. It's a little dangerous. I'm sure someone is looking for the pieces of the sword. And I don't want you caught up in the crossfire,' James said with a slight smile.

'That's ageism.' Francois had a defiant look in his eye.

What a surprise.

Francois's slender frame tensed as if to wind up for a second round. 'I'm fit for someone my age. And I can handle blood. I still get called in by the police to do autopsies on special occasions.'

There was no way his grandfather would sit in a nearby

patisserie and eat a croissant and sip coffee while James searched a chateau closed for refurbishment. Ever since James could remember, his grandfather had been addicted to visiting chateaux and abbeys. Every chance he had, Francois dragged James and his grandmother Valerie along for walking tours. That was the risk James had taken when he asked his grandfather to drive from Poitiers in central western France to Gare du Nord in Paris, and then the one-hour drive to the city of Pierrefonds.

James contemplated the inevitable wrath of his grandmother if anything were to happen to the short elderly man sitting next to him.

She's going to kill me and then bring me back to clean up the mess.

'James, are you listening?' Francois took his eyes off the road and glared at James, jolting him back to reality. 'You need me to come with you because my friend Jean Philippe de Benoist is the conservateur of the chateau. It's closed for refurbishment. He will not let you in without me present.'

'*Papi*, he knows me. He always stays with us in Poitiers for New Year.'

'It's already been decided—there's no use changing things now.' The doctor waved his finger at James as he turned in to a car park along the street, reached down, and pulled the handbrake.

James jolted forward in his seat and almost hit his head on the dashboard.

———

A CHILL LINGERED in the air as James walked along the wooden pathway of the darkened catacombs of Chateau de Pierrefonds. It was three forty-five in the afternoon. James had spent the last ninety minutes searching the chateau with his grandfather, but he had nothing to show for it. As James walked along the arched pathway, he paused and looked into the shadows at the effigies of the former kings of France.

James stepped over the thin guardrail, took the yellow hard hat off his head, placed it on the closest effigy, and walked among the sculptures.

'No,' Francois whispered from the pathway.

'It has to be here.' James continued to weave in and out of the graves, looking at the faces from the past.

'You said that before.'

'I won't touch anything.' James pre-empted the inevitable conversation as he turned towards the pathway. '*Papi*?' James said as he looked around the room.

James ran toward the pathway, weaving in and out of the effigies. He froze and looked at the ground, then looked down the path toward the next room. James's heart raced as he looked in the opposite direction.

'This one is missing everything from the neck up,' Francois called out from the shadows behind him.

James sighed and followed the voice into the shadows, to the last row of effigies. The elderly Frenchman was crouched down and squinting through his thick, red-framed glasses at the faint writing on the plaque.

James rolled his eyes. His grandfather was too close to the effigy. Any moment now he was going to reach out and pat it. He couldn't take his grandfather anywhere. One time at the Louvre his grandfather patted one of the Great Sphinx of Tanis.

'I cannot read this.' Francois waved his hand at the sign. 'It must be around here somewhere.' He spoke over his shoulder as he walked up the row towards the back of the catacombs. Francois reached out and patted the foot of one of the nearby effigies.

James stared at the headless figure in front of him. The break was clean.

It's almost as if it was deliberate.

A flicker of metal caught his eye, and he bent over. Nestled between the base of the effigy and the slab of concrete underneath was a piece of aged metal no longer than the length of his hand. With his nails, James scratched at the metal until it wiggled free from its concrete prison. He held the piece of the sword in his hand and drew it closer towards his face so he could view the word etched on its side. It was the second missing piece, but was it enough for a trade?

From the far corner of the catacombs, James heard what sounded like the rolling of cement. He looked up towards the sound. Silence filled the room as an intense wave of pain permeated the back of James's head. The room started to spin, and his body lunged forward. As the catacomb floor raced towards him, James hit his forehead on the effigy.

A sharp pain shot across James's forehead as the ache in the back of his head increased. The frames of his thick, black spectacles dug into his cheekbones. He tried to pick himself up, but something or someone was pulling him down to the ground. The room continued to spin faster as his eyelids grew heavy.

A pair of warm hands turned him over to his back. Towering over him in the shadows and blocking the hazy lights was a familiar forbidding figure. As he tried to resist the urge to close his eyes and sleep, a pair of bright blue eyes came into view.

'I knew it was y—' James said as the intruder's fist came hurling towards him.

THIRTY-ONE

WEDNESDAY: 10:49 P.M.

THE SEARCH for the pieces of the sword was unsuccessful, and James had nothing to bargain with to set Valentine and Elizabeth free, other than the small piece collected from Elizabeth's office. All he had was a headache and a graze across his forehead, where Maximilian had smashed his head into the effigy and escaped with the piece of the sword.

He must be working with someone. It's the only plausible reason for him getting to Pierrefonds so quickly.

James wrinkled his brow and felt a sharp sting from the graze. The pain was most likely from the Betadine solution that Margaret had insisted on bathing the graze in before she applied a massive plaster from the first-aid box. His grandfather had done the same thing a few hours earlier, moments before James boarded the Eurostar. Now, he looked like a giant idiot with a large white patch on his forehead.

As per usual, another ivory piece of paper had made its way into James's inbox, and no one in the newsroom knew how it got there. This time, the note was brief. It contained the location of the drop-off, and it was just as he expected. The site was a remote location on the outskirts of Northampton, a place he had seen on one of his many train trips between

130

Birmingham City University—where he completed his master's degree in multiplatform and mobile journalism—and Northampton. James had taken the trip several times over a few weeks for interviews with the former editor of the *Northampton Tribune.*

James looked at the small piece of the sword in his hand that he had retrieved from Elizabeth's office. It was still sharp and cut into the first layer of skin on his palm. Was it enough to trade for Valentine? His eyes glazed over as he placed the sword fragment in the tissue on his desk, then leaned over, pulled at the top drawer, lifted a small white envelope out, and opened it.

The envelope contained a picture of Valentine that had come with the ransom note the previous day.

Where is he hiding you?

James stared at the picture in his hand.

'Please tell me you notified the police,' Josh said from over James's shoulder, disturbing the silence of his office.

James jumped and looked up at Josh, who seemed to have materialised from out of nowhere. 'Yes, the police have the original and the note.' James studied the photograph. 'Not that it's doing me any good.'

Josh leaned over his shoulder and pointed towards the lower left-hand corner of the photograph. 'You know, there's something familiar about that picture, but I can't put my finger on it.'

'Me too. I think I've seen the floor somewhere, but it could be from several buildings around town.'

'Really?'

James sighed and placed the photo on his desk. He leaned to the side, rested his head in his right hand, and stared at the computer screen. 'Stay here while I check the layout.' James clicked his mouse a few times and opened the InDesign file.

James flipped through the file of the next morning's issue. He stopped on each page, paying careful attention to each banner headline. Then it dawned on him. But it was too simple. Could Maximilian be that stupid?

'The NMA used to have a similar pattern on the main floor before they renovated the building. They were closed for four months during autumn and winter a few years back. I had planned on taking Valentine to the museum on a date, but I didn't check to see if it was open.' James stared at the computer screen.

Josh turned towards James and held his finger in the air as if deep in thought. 'They probably didn't renovate the entire building, including offices or archives.'

In a few simple clicks, James was staring at a sea of images of the Northampton Museum of Anthropology from the summer of 2013. It was as he had expected—halfway down the page, a familiar pattern came into view. Valentine had been there the entire time. His heart sank. Why did he not check the museum?

James shot up from his chair, grabbed the jacket draped over the back, and sprinted towards the front door.

'What about the layout?' Josh yelled as he clutched the back of James's chair.

'It's fine. They've submitted everything early for once,' James said over his shoulder as he dashed out of the office.

As he sprinted across the newsroom, the words of his grandfather drifted into his mind. *Always come prepared for all eventualities.*

THIRTY-TWO

THE NEO-GOTHIC ARCHITECTURE of the NMA towered over him as he ascended the stairs and took a left. James paused. The front door was ajar. It turned out that breaking and entering would be easier than he had imagined.

The gods are finally smiling upon me.

He trudged towards the front door and pushed it open, hoping the large, heavy door wouldn't make a sound and disturb the silence of the sleeping museum.

As James walked through the foyer, past the second set of doors, and went into the darkness of the museum, he surveyed the maze of anthropological artefacts. No security guard was in sight. But there was no time to question the security choices of the small museum. The ransom was due by midnight and must be dropped off at a location on the outskirts of Northampton. James had less than an hour to find the women.

He strolled through the maze of displays, up the central staircase to the mezzanine level, and down the hall towards the enormous set of double doors that led to the administration offices. As the door opened, a sharp creak sounded in the darkness of the museum. He looked down the corridor. No light was on, not even under any of the doors. James looked at the floor, which differed from the photo.

He sighed and walked back through the mezzanine level, down the stairs, and onto the main floor. James shuffled through the maze of displays towards the back section of the building. He had assumed the door to the archives would be at the rear.

Then it dawned on him. The archives might be in a different location somewhere across town, and he was in the wrong place, wasting time. As he contemplated this new reality, he tripped over a heavy object on the floor near a display.

I hope it's not expensive.

James pulled out his phone, clicked the home button, and used the glow from the screen to light his way. He froze as his eyes lingered at his feet.

On the ground lay a wiry, grey-haired man wearing a dark-blue uniform with a gold-plated badge that read "Charlie"— the first casualty of the evening. That answered James's question about the night staff and the open doors.

Perfect.

He knelt, rested two fingers on the side of the man's neck, and felt the coolness of his dark skin.

Merde.

The old man looked as if he was in his late sixties; this wasn't the retirement a man like him should enjoy at his stage in life.

James's phone buzzed in his hand—an incoming text. He glanced at the first line of the notification on the screen. It was a last-minute article for editing and layout approval, this one about a new threat to the security of internet banking.

Merde.

James checked his watch. Out of the corner of his eye,

thanks to the glow from his screen, James saw a white door with a sign labelled "Staff Only."

James sprinted across the floor and turned the handle. It was unlocked. He stepped onto the landing, clicked the torch icon on the home screen, and looked down the staircase.

THIRTY-THREE

A FAINT WHIMPER came from within the darkness of the lower-ground archives. James inched down the hall as he listened to the sound, trying to determine its exact location.

'Valentine?' James paused and listened for a response. A whimper echoed down the darkness of the hallway once more, but this time, it sounded closer. His heart raced. James held his phone and shone the torchlight beaming out just above the camera lens. His eyes fixed on the sign that flashed up on the screen—less than 10% battery.

Perfect.

James struck the button on the warning message and powered down the torch. He focused his attention on the door in front of him. A chill darted up his arm as he grabbed the handle. His heart raced as he pushed the door open. James stepped into the room and waited for his eyes to adjust to the darkness. He was running out of time, and he didn't want to keep betting on his presence going unnoticed.

Light from the street level beamed through a corner of the window and across the shelves filled with tagged artefacts. It was just like Elizabeth's office. As he walked across the room towards the small window, James saw the source of the sound.

As he'd expected, Valentine was gagged and tied to a chair. Her skin was pale, and her green eyes were filled with fear. He sprinted across the room, knelt in front of her, and pulled down her gag. James leaned in and caressed her cold, dry lips.

He pulled away and looked into her eyes, holding on to the chair. 'I'm sorry,' James said as he stood and leaned over her.

'You shouldn't have come here,' Valentine said in a frantic tone.

'What did he do to you?' James leaned in to kiss her again.

'I tried to make a run for it, but he was too strong,' Valentine sobbed.

James looked into her widened eyes. He turned around to see a familiar six-foot frame step out of the shadows. In the darkness, the man seemed more intimidating, and his muscular frame towered over James.

'Maximilian?' James said as the figure stood in the shadows.

As the figure stepped into the light, a familiar head of scruffy brown hair came into view.

'Sorry, I thought you were Maximilian. Help me untie Valentine, then we'll find Elizabeth. I know she's here somewhere.' James turned around and glanced up at Alistair, who stood watching with his hands in his pockets. Then the penny dropped. His eyes widened. It had been Alistair all along. Everything Alistair had done up to now was orchestrated—it was a show, and he fell for it, just as he was supposed to.

Alistair grinned. 'You've finally put the pieces together. I was wondering if you were ever going to figure it out.'

In that moment, James knew he was trapped between the lanky figure and Valentine. He couldn't resist whatever Alistair had planned for him. Well, not at first. Alistair grabbed James by his bicep and dragged him towards the door. He was surprisingly strong. The man appeared to never have graced the walls of a gym, but James had been wrong about that assumption—very wrong.

'All you had to do was pay the ransom. That's it. Instead, you made the mistake of bursting in here like a 007 movie.' Alistair continued to stride towards the door. 'You've made a huge mistake.'

James realised no one knew where he was except for Josh from Layout. In a moment of panic, James looked around the room for a way out or something to hold on to that would slow Alistair down. Out of the corner of his eye, he spotted an old vase at the edge of a metal shelving unit. It was within his grasp.

James reached for the vase. He pulled away from Alistair's grip as he was dragged towards the door. It was as if the man couldn't feel the resistance.

James's fingers clutched the top of the vase. He pulled his arm back and struck Alistair over the head in one swift, catapulting motion.

THIRTY-FOUR

WEDNESDAY: 11:29 P.M.

JAMES BROKE free from Alistair's grip. Moments later, James was at the top of the stairs, millimetres away from freedom. The lanky nerd grabbed him by the ankle. As James glanced down at Alistair, for the first time, James saw the icy stare in Alistair's eyes. There was something menacing about the gaze. But what he couldn't figure out was his motive. Did he want the sword for himself? Was this his motive for murder, kidnapping, and theft? James was missing something. *Merde. I'm still too far away.*

He looked down at Alistair again.

In one swift motion, James kicked his right leg back and struck Alistair in the nose with his brown leather boot. Alistair stifled a groan as he immediately released his grip on James's ankle. James sprinted through the door and across the museum floor. He was free.

A pair of cold, large hands grabbed James by the shoulders, then slammed him against the display cabinet, shattering the glass panel, exposing a series of tribal spears to the atmosphere of the room. He pushed against Alistair, but the man didn't budge, not even a millimetre. James felt like an overambitious ant, trying to push a cupcake into his anthill.

Blood trickled down the side of Alistair's face from his hairline. He wiped his forehead. Alistair raised his perfectly sculptured eyebrow at James and smirked. He was trapped and at Alistair's mercy, but he would not go quietly.

James smiled to himself as he set a spear free from the cabinet behind him. As he drew the spear closer, James cut his wrist on the shattered glass on the edge of the display case. Alistair's eyes snapped to the tribal spear in James's hand, and he groaned. He released his grip on James and clutched the end of the long spear instead. James pulled the spear towards him and tried to shake Alistair's hand free. Only one option was left.

James released his grip on the tribal spear. In one swift motion, the butt of the spear propelled forward and struck Alistair in the face. Alistair clutched his cheek as James seized another spear from the display.

'Not that.' Alistair directed James to put the object back where he found it. 'It's real. Not all of this is, but that item costs several million pounds and is not replaceable.'

James dropped the spear and dashed towards the stairs that led to the mezzanine level. He turned around, finding Alistair close behind.

'Suddenly grown a conscience?' James pushed a tribal statue on top of his opponent.

Alistair grimaced as he rolled the statue off him and onto the floor. James panicked as his foe picked up his pace and strode towards him. He raced around the museum floor, then made a beeline towards a cabinet full of swords. Out of the corner of his eye, James saw the spear lying on the ground. He picked it up and threw it towards the glass.

It bounced off.

'It's made of wood, genius,' Alistair said with a hint of laughter.

As Alistair approached, James punched the glass. Upon impact, the glass shattered across the floor and rained over him. James reached his bloodied hand into the cabinet, pulled out a sword, and pointed it at Alistair's chest.

'Do it,' he taunted James. 'You can't. Can you?' Alistair kicked James in the stomach.

James fell backwards and released his grip on the sword. Both he and the sword fell to the floor. Alistair picked the blade up as James crawled over to the display case and pulled out another sword. He rushed across the floor, looking for a place to shield himself from Alistair's blade. James froze as he felt the edge of a sword digging into his back. James dropped his sword, faced Alistair, and placed his hands in the air. Alistair lowered his sword and grabbed James by the collar.

James seized the opportunity and kicked the sword out of Alistair's hand. The weapon flew across the museum floor. Alistair shook his hand, then clenched it into a fist, pulled back, and in one swift motion struck James in the jaw. As James fought back, Alistair pushed him against another cabinet. Out of the corner of James's eye, he saw Alistair's dark-grey jacket lying across a chair on the far side of the museum, a black bag protruding from a pocket.

The sword. He brought it with him. What an idiot.

Alistair looked toward James's gaze. James pushed Alistair off him and sprinted across the floor, but the tall man reached the chair first. He pulled the broken sword out of the bag and pointed the blade at James's chest.

'You should have stayed out of this.' Alistair inched closer to James.

James stepped back and tripped over the tribal statue before he plummeted towards the floor. 'And just stand back and watch you murder colleagues and museum staff, lie and steal? All for a sword.'

Alistair scowled as he towered over him and gripped the broken sword with his fist. 'Is that what you think this is about? This sword represents my entire life's work—years of research. I've lobbied the North Cornwall council for years seeking permission to dig.' Alistair's face flushed a shade of crimson as he hunched over James.

A sharp pain shot through James's lower back as he struggled to breathe.

'It was I who suggested to that imbecile of a caretaker at Tintagel to dig in that section of the land,' Alistair bellowed. 'After he dug and found a hint of metal, the caretaker rang his niece, Elizabeth, instead of me. When I found out, I persuaded Elizabeth that she needed my expertise. Now, she's taking all the credit. So when I was given a better offer—rightful credit, a book deal, tours at the best museums—I naturally jumped at it. Later, I realised the offer came with strings attached and loopholes that would only benefit the investor. So I took matters into my own hands. With Elizabeth behind bars, I can just seize credit for all my hard work.'

Alistair raised the broken sword to prepare for a potentially fatal blow. It would take only one. As Alistair lowered the sword, James struggled to pull his weary body away from his attacker.

THIRTY-FIVE

TWO GREY-HAIRED MEN wearing dark-blue uniforms pinned themselves to the backs of two pillars that were supporting the archways on the upper mezzanine level. The floor was shrouded in darkness. A short, round man with a moustache leaned to the left to get a better view of the fight that had broken out in the main level of the museum below. He looked across at his long-time colleague and pointed towards the oak-stained doors that led to the administration office.

Greg shook his head in protest. Bob sighed, raised his left hand, made a telephoning gesture, and glared at Greg. It was the right thing to do. The dark grey-haired man shook his head and moved his lips and mouthed the word no.

'You realise we're next?' Bob inched over to the nearest pillar and grabbed Greg by his collar.

Greg folded his arms across his chest.

'No matter how this plays out, he will find us. Then we're toast. If we call the police, at least there will be people on their way to help us.' Bob pulled his colleague down the hall in the darkness. 'We both saw what happened to Charlie. I will not stand around and wait for another guy to die tonight. We need a panic button, of sorts,' Bob said as Greg resisted being dragged towards the approaching double doors.

———

BOB LEANED on the reception desk; he was on hold. It had been only ten minutes since he dragged Greg into the offices on the upper mezzanine level, and he was already having regrets. He could sense Greg thinking, "I told you so." But Bob didn't want to leave his friend behind, no matter how irritating he could be and no matter how tempting the idea seemed.

'They've put me on hold.' Bob placed his hand over the receiver. He held his finger in the air as a voice came through on the line.

'I work the night shift at the NMA, and I'd like to report a murder, fight, and potential theft. Two men are fighting among the anthropological artefacts on the main floor of the museum. A light-brown-haired guy with a thick French accent in a grey suit, and a tall, scruffy-haired man.'

Bob paused as he listened to the officer on the other end of the line.

'I don't know. He looks like a tall, aristocratic nerd to me.' Bob looked up at Greg and waved his hand in frustration.

All he wanted was for the police to show up before anyone else died or destroyed millions of pounds' worth of irreplaceable artefacts. Instead, the police seemed more concerned with physical descriptions of the suspects.

They're not as good as they used to be.

'He works here. I'm sure of it.' Greg folded his arms and raised his eyebrows at Bob, interrupting the conversation.

Bob hung up the phone and looked at his colleague. 'They'll be here in five minutes. Fingers crossed the aristocratic nerd doesn't find us first.'

THIRTY-SIX

THURSDAY: 12:09 A.M.

ALISTAIR WATCHED the pain build in James's eyes as he lay on the museum floor. But Alistair had a job to do. He needed to collect the missing pieces of the sword and deliver them, despite the long list of people who kept getting in his way. It was almost as if the man lying on the ground before him had a thirst for trouble and wasn't satisfied unless he was up to his eyeballs in it. As Alistair pulled out the broken sword, James arched his back and gripped his thigh, and looked up at the bloodied, broken end of the sword. Blood trickled out of his wound as James gritted his teeth.

Perhaps out of naivety, Alistair hoped this would be the last job he had to do to protect his life's work and his professional reputation. But part of him knew better. There would be others who desired to seek the legendary sword and come to claim it. Then there was his dear friend, Maximilian. The investor had him between a rock and a hard place. His business partner was desperate, and desperate men could not be trusted. So, there was one more person he had to rid himself of, but he needed to get creative about that. Alistair leaned down and wiped the blood across James's grey suit jacket. As Alistair got up from his kneeling position, he saw the look of terror in James's eyes.

The sound of tyres screeching to a halt broke his concentration. Someone had called the police—he needed to leave. There was only one entrance he could take. The secret entrance that he had discovered, a month ago, when he first planned the events.

Alistair looked across the room towards the half-open wooden doors that led to the foyer. He pulled out a black drawstring bag from his dark-grey jacket and opened it. He pulled out several layers of crushed-up tissue paper and wrapped the sword. A pool of blood formed under James's thigh as Alistair glanced over to see if James was following him. James's thick blond eyelashes flickered, revealing a hint of blue-green before they closed.

Alistair placed the sword into the bag and trudged across the museum floor towards the closed "Staff Only" door, dragging James and leaving a trail of blood behind him.

THIRTY-SEVEN

A SHARP PAIN dug into James's wrists, waking him from his slumber. As his eyes opened, the blurry haze of a familiar ceiling came into view. He was still in the Northampton Museum of Anthropology, but this room was different. On his right were shelves lined with tribal artefacts from lost civilisations. Across the room, with his ear to the door, stood Alistair.

Clang. A loud noise echoed through the museum floor above. Alistair's eyes darted across the room to the wall behind him. James followed his gaze to the small, hazy glass window at the top of the wall. A faint yellow light from a streetlamp shone through.

A second loud *clang* echoed through the museum. Then, like a frightened animal, Alistair opened the door and dashed into the hall, leaving James behind, tied and bound.

Thankful that for once he had heeded his grandfather's advice, James tugged at the right cuff of his white business shirt. After a few strong yanks at the fabric, the material tore, revealing a tiny blade inelegantly sewn in hours before. He had removed it from a sharpener left behind on Valentine's desk. Digging his short fingernail between the blade and the cuff of his shirt, James pulled it free and cut his ties while keeping an eye on the door.

Far off in the distance, James listened to Alistair's footsteps move further away. A door slammed. Was he really leaving?

In less than a few minutes, James had cut the rope around his wrists and feet and then pulled off the fabric around his mouth. He was free. But would Alistair return, or was he on the run?

———

JAMES LEANED his slender frame against the door frame of the opened storeroom. Through a blurry haze, he looked down the hall of the archives. The room spun as he loosened his grey tie. Blood streamed down his thigh and left a trail as he staggered along the corridor. Walking the final few metres through the maze of archive rooms would be agonising. But he would never make it unless he slowed the bleeding.

He tugged at his now-loosened tie and freed it from his neck. Then he bent over and tied it around the top part of his thigh, above the stab wound. Thankfully, Alistair missed the femoral artery and veins. All he had to do was release Elizabeth and Valentine from their bonds and bring them up to the main floor of the museum. The room spun faster as he tightened the tie and hobbled the final few metres towards the next archive room.

———

AFTER NINE MINUTES of pure agony, James blinked the tears out of his eyelashes as he hovered over Valentine's chair and braced himself for the pain to come. Every slight movement brought a fresh wave of pain. Each wave was deeper and stronger than the one before.

'He's gone.' James looked at Valentine and reached down to untie her bonds.

'You're bleeding.'

'I think a noise within the museum spooked Alistair, then he made a quick getaway.'

'Who's Alistair?'

'He's the tall, lanky guy with messy brown hair. You know, the guy who's been holding you down here.'

Valentine stared off into the distance and shrugged. 'I never saw his face. He lurked in the shadows.'

'We need to get out of here.'

'You can barely stand,' she said.

James winced as he crouched down and untied the bonds around her legs. 'There's someone else locked down here. I need to find her.'

'You need to go to the hospital.'

James sighed as he looked up at Valentine. 'I'm not leaving here without her.'

'Why can't you listen to me for once?'

'I can't just leave her down here.' James reached out his hand to help her up.

'Frenchmen. You're all the same.' Valentine rose from the chair and put her right arm under James's arm to support his upper body.

'I know you've been down here for days and you're probably tired, but I need you to help me through the hallways.' James placed his arm around her shoulder, leaned on her for support, and staggered towards the door.

'I thought I heard people arguing. Maybe this morning. I'm sure one of them was that guy,' Valentine said as they reached the doorway.

James tilted his head to the right as they stepped into the hallway together. There was so much he wanted to say to her, but none of the words seemed to make up for what she had endured over the last few days. His guilt was almost unbearable, but it had to wait. So he did the only thing he knew to do and buried himself in the task at hand. James paused at every doorway. He thumped the wall and called out Elizabeth's name.

'James, you'll never find her this way. You need to go to a hospital and call the police and let them find her.' Valentine pointed towards the stairs.

'No.' James leaned against the wall and staggered down the hall alone. 'I'm the reason she's here. All of this is my fault. I have to find her.' He bashed the last door.

He waited in the silence. As he turned around, he heard a faint, muffled cry nearby.

THIRTY-EIGHT

THURSDAY: 12:39 A.M.

ANWAR, Chan, and a backup crew crept through the museum entry, holding torches to light the way. Holding his left hand up, Anwar paused. He listened but heard nothing. The museum was asleep. Anwar signalled for a group to go up the staircase and search the mezzanine level.

He stopped in the middle of the entry to the museum floor, pulled out his phone, and tapped the home key. On the screen was a series of numbers. He struck the screen again, hit Speaker, and waited for the dial tone. But the museum remained silent.

Why did he turn off his phone?

Anwar pounded the redial button once more, then slid it inside his stab-proof vest.

As they inched through the museum, his tiny torch highlighted a trail of broken pottery and tribal poles scattered on the floor. A pool of blood, followed by a smudged path, pointed towards the back of the museum floor.

'Oh, shit.' Anwar looked at the ground.

James, what have you done?

'That belongs to James, doesn't it?' Chan said as he caught up with the detective.

Anwar closed his eyes and sighed. He should have kept surveillance on James. The Frenchman had a nose for trouble.

'Chan, you appear to have been right all along.' Anwar inched around the trail of blood towards the back of the museum.

'Ah, Anwar.' Chan waved his torch around and shone it towards a back corner of the room, highlighting the wiry frame of an elderly security guard slumped against an exhibit filled with swords. He knelt and checked the man's pulse.

'Call Dr Deschamps. He's on call tonight.' Anwar looked up at Chan.

As Chan pulled his radio off his shoulder, the white door at the back of the building swung open. Valentine and Elizabeth staggered out with James leaning on their shoulders for support. James's grey tie was fastened with a knot around his upper left thigh. Blood streamed down his leg and soaked into the grey material of his trousers.

Anwar sprinted across the room towards James as he collapsed to the floor, bringing both of the women down with him. Anwar leaned over him, then rolled James onto his back. James's eyelashes flickered, then remained still. The detective looked across at Valentine. Her green eyes were dull and scared.

'Rogers, sit the women on the stairs away from the trail of evidence,' Anwar barked out as he slapped the pale skin of James's cheeks and screamed out, 'Ambulance, now!'

Anwar looked up at Chan. 'Get me the first-aid kit out of the car.'

A tall, ginger-haired, uniformed police officer walked Valentine and Elizabeth over to the stairs near the door, and Anwar sighed as James lay on the floor. James didn't move or make a sound. *Not again.*

'Next, we're going after Alistair,' Anwar barked over his shoulder.

THIRTY-NINE

AFTER A TWENTY-SIX-MINUTE CAR ride and a further nineteen minutes waiting around in the cold, isolated aerodrome on the outskirts of Northampton, Alistair ambled along the tarmac towards the private jet. The cool wind blew straight through his dark-grey jacket, causing him to shiver. He was mere minutes away from freedom.

But he was not a fool. Tucked safely in a hiding spot known only to him was Excalibur, waiting to be discovered once again by him at a more appropriate time. After witnessing Maximilian's misfortune, Alistair was more determined to ensure the investor would not get the better of him. As he gazed across the tarmac towards the private jet, he realised the staff had not lowered its stairs.

Imbeciles.

Alistair shook his head and turned to trek back to the aerodrome building. Then, seemingly out of nowhere, Anwar, Chan and a team of police officers, all wearing matching, stab-proof vests, burst out of the door and ran towards him.

'Police,' Anwar cried out over the loud hum of the jet engines.

Alistair whirled around. His heart raced. He was trapped

between the closed door of the jet and an army of police officers. The investor must have sensed he was being screwed over. *Shit.*

Raising his hands, Alistair whirled around to face the army of police officers. It was his only option. Running was a futile endeavour.

Chan unclipped a set of handcuffs off his belt as he followed Anwar across the tarmac.

'I'm arresting you on suspicion of the murder of Pippa Baker, the kidnapping of Valentine Charlet and Elizabeth James, and the theft of a Celtic Sword on loan to the Northampton Museum of Anthropology, catalogue number NMA-642901A. You do not have to say anything, but it may harm your defence if you do not mention, when questioned, something you later rely on in court. Anything you do say may be given in evidence.' Anwar directed Alistair across the tarmac towards the airport.

———

ALISTAIR WALKED into the police station with Chan gripping his bicep. The scruffy, brown-haired man flinched as the short police officer tightened his grip. Chan stopped in front of the reception desk. They were greeted with a warm smile.

The curvy, dark-skinned woman in her early forties looked up at Alistair, then over at the constable.

'Don't I get a call?' Alistair stared at Chan.

The PC smirked as he reached across the reception desk, picked up a small office phone, and pulled it towards Alistair. 'Be my guest.'

Alistair picked up the receiver and dialled an international number located in the French Riviera.

'I guess you probably know that number by heart by now,' Chan said.

As he listened to the dial tone, Alistair felt the watchful eyes of the PC fix themselves on him. Not that it was any surprise, but by entering the station, he had kissed his right to privacy goodbye. The fewer words Alistair said, the better. The last thing he needed was to serve himself to the police on a silver platter. So, it was decided that he would call his father, who would contact criminal barrister QC Bradley Evans. Calling him from a police station phone was practically an admission of guilt, and only an idiot would do that—he was not an idiot.

'I need you to make that call. The call I spoke to you about earlier. I'm at the Northampton District Police Station.' Alistair clunked the receiver down and faced Chan, who was standing next to him at the reception desk.

'This way. I need to fingerprint you before putting you in the holding cell.' Chan paused and looked up at Alistair. 'I hope you called your lawyer.'

FORTY

A BRIGHT WHITE light shone into James's blue-green eyes as he opened them. It was too bright. He closed his eyes and smelt the familiar fragrance of disinfectant mixed with Betadine. The smell of the yellowish-brown liquid reminded him of his grandparents. His grandfather was a pathologist, and his grandmother was an OBGYN. Betadine was his grandfather's favourite product, and a bottle of it went everywhere with him—the result of an "expect the best and prepare for the worst" mentality. Another habit to thank his grandparents for.

A few moments later, James felt a warm hand on his arm as the metal trolley he was on stopped rolling. James opened his eyes to find Harry Lancaster at his side.

Oh, merde. Now I'm in trouble.

James's eyesight blurred.

'The paper,' he whispered.

'Really?' Harry looked down at James. 'This is your biggest problem right now?'

'There's one more article to edit,' James said. 'It came through last-minute on my phone.'

'James,' Harry said with a hint of sympathy. 'I think I

know how to get an edition ready for publication. Did I not accompany you on a few of your first late nights?'

James nodded as the emergency doctors rolled him through the double doors from the waiting area to the A&E.

'Don't worry about the next few editions,' Harry told James as the doors closed and the trolley stopped rolling.

James pulled out his phone and hit the home button. There were no new messages.

'Mr Lalonde, I'll keep that safe for you,' the doctor said as he pushed a mask onto James's face.

James felt lightheaded as the doctor grabbed his phone. The room spun, and he took a few more deep breaths. It was as if he were floating on a cloud. Whatever the doctor was administering to him through the mask was good; it was fantastic.

For the first time in the last few hours, James felt pain-free. His eyelids grew heavy. There was no use fighting it anymore. As his eyes closed, his world filled with darkness.

FORTY-ONE

THURSDAY: 5:59 A.M.

JAMES COULDN'T SHAKE the thought as he limped down the hall towards her room. The doctor had pleaded with him to stay and rest, but he felt obliged to tell her the truth. To warn her of Alistair's motives and the potential involvement of his business partner, Maximilian, in the events of the last few days. She had the right to know.

As James walked down the hall, the cool breeze from the hospital air-conditioning shot straight through the blue surgical shirt and trousers the doctor had given him moments before James discharged himself. The clear plastic bag with his bloodstained clothes swung with the rhythm of his stride. James stopped as he saw the room number on the white door ahead of him. He patted his phone through the side pocket of the blue cotton trousers. The door was ajar.

Through the narrow gap between the door and the frame, James watched Maximilian lean in and embrace Elizabeth.

She pushed him back and glared at him.

Maximilian hung his head. 'I'm sorry. I was never going to hurt you with those pliers. But I needed you to believe I was, so you would give me the information about where you hid the pieces. Alistair was clearly after them too, which meant the investor was getting desperate.'

'Oh, and that makes everything better.' Elizabeth narrowed her eyes. 'Why didn't you set me free?'

'Are you serious?' Maximilian waved his arm in the air. 'That would make everything worse. I had planned on coming back for you after I had all the pieces. But James got to you first. I don't know why Alistair didn't kill you all. Especially after what he did to Pippa.' Maximilian's eyes glazed over as his voice broke.

'Sorry, I thought it was you all along. I really misjudged you,' she said as Maximilian adjusted his posture and sat on the edge of her bed.

'It shocked me to discover that Alistair had kidnapped you. But, now that I've had a chance to think, it doesn't surprise me,' Maximilian said in a rehearsed tone.

Elizabeth hung her head. 'You mean because of the domestic violence order?' She sobbed. 'I swear I was drunk. I didn't mean to hurt him, and I'm trying to stop drinking.'

Maximilian grimaced. 'You believe you were violent towards Alistair?'

'Yes,' she sobbed. 'Alistair kept it to himself. I think he was embarrassed.'

Maximilian's mouth hung open. 'Sure, you have a bit of a temper and you're bossy, but you were never violent towards Alistair. It was the other way around.'

Elizabeth shook her head. 'No, it was me.'

'I was there that day. Yes, you have an issue with alcohol. But that started after your miscarriage. During a function, you caught Alistair flirting with someone, and you had a huge fight. After everyone left, I could hear you both screaming upstairs. When I heard a loud bang, I came upstairs to find that Alistair had thrown you against the wall.' Maximilian grabbed her hand. 'That's why the main bedroom was renovated.'

'But there's a DVO out against me.'

Maximilian sighed. 'There's no DVO. And you believed him because your memory is hazy and probably fractured due to the alcohol and trauma you've experienced. He's the one with the issues with violence.'

'But he had bruises. And so did I.'

'Ever heard of a theatre bruise kit? Alistair has one. He did theatre at university, remember?'

Elizabeth stared off into the distance. 'What about the other woman? Who was she?'

'I was surprised when Alistair kidnapped Valentine, James's girlfriend. He kept a close eye on James when he showed up at the crime scene and then the estate.' Maximilian grabbed her hands.

'You knew about his girlfriend?' Elizabeth moved closer and looked into Maximilian's eyes.

James slumped against the wall for support and clutched his leg. With trembling hands, he pulled out his smartphone. He brushed his finger along the screen and hit the camera icon, then he tapped the large red record button and continued to listen to the conversation.

'Yes, but I have my reasons. Our American investor has been holding my parents hostage for over fourteen months. I have to do that guy's bidding.'

'I realise that.' Elizabeth placed her hand on his chest and created a distance between them. 'That's why I hid the pieces of the sword during the excavation stage. That's why the NMA doesn't know about the full sword, just the biggest piece. I was worried that your insistence on bringing that man on board would put my professional reputation at risk. And, I thought, you might deliver the sword to him, even if it was to get your parents back. I'm sorry. But I never imagined that his involvement would cause Pippa's death.'

Maximilian shook his head. 'Hiding the pieces was a bit

overdramatic. How could you possibly know that someone would steal the sword?'

'I could tell the American wanted to add the sword to his personal collection. I knew it's more than just "a love of history," as he put it.'

'Why didn't you tell me all of this?'

'How could I trust you?' Elizabeth raised her eyebrows at Maximilian. 'You have a terrible reputation. And what about the Egypt incident? Everyone thinks you're a tomb raider.'

'We'll figure this out. I'll get my parents back and give this guy what he wants, and find the sword that Alistair hid.' Maximilian took a deep breath.

'It won't work out that way. Whatever you do, it will never be enough.'

'Don't worry. I'll figure something out.'

'Really?' Elizabeth glared at him with her big brown eyes.

'Yes, I'm sure the investor will pull a few strings and get Alistair off the hook.'

'God, I hope not.' Elizabeth settled back against the elevated mattress and grabbed Maximilian's left hand. 'And James will never accept that. I don't know him well, but he seems determined and not the type to let something like this go. I got a taste of it in my office before I was kidnapped. He won't forgive Alistair for this. Or you, if he suspects you're involved. And besides, I'm not sure if I want to see Alistair get away with this. He murdered Pippa.'

'Don't worry about it.' Maximilian kissed Elizabeth on the forehead.

Elizabeth pulled away. 'How can you stand by Alistair after all of this? After Pippa and Excalibur. You've worked hard to find that sword, just like I did.'

Maximilian sighed. 'He's like a brother to me. He stood by me when no one else would.'

Elizabeth looked away. 'Don't you care about Pippa?'

'I was dating Pippa for well over a year. She was the first

person to find out about my parents. She was super supportive.' Maximilian turned and stared out the window. 'I told her not to get involved several times. But Pippa thought if she stole the sword, she could swap it in exchange for my parents.'

'And how do you know that?'

'It was an idea she came up with a couple of months ago. I told her it was too risky, and that she should leave it be.' Maximilian sighed. 'At first, I thought she had listened. You know the rest. I can't talk about this anymore.'

James took a silent deep breath as he tapped the record button and slipped the phone back into his pocket. He couldn't bear to listen to their conversation any longer. It was too painful. If he had stayed out of it and let Anwar charge her with Pippa's murder, then Valentine would have been at home in Paris with her parents and avoided the entire kidnapping. James's chest tightened as he wondered where Valentine was at this moment.

Would she return to Paris? Was there any hope of changing her mind or getting to say goodbye? His heart raced as he pushed away from the wall and walked down the hall. He couldn't bear to witness the reunion a second longer. With every stride down the hallway and away from Elizabeth's room, the more he wanted revenge. A pit formed in the depths of his stomach as he contemplated his next move.

FORTY-TWO

THURSDAY: 7:01 A.M.

A SHARP PAIN shot deep into James's thigh. The morphine had worn off. With every step up the stairs and towards his bedroom, it intensified. It wasn't unbearable yet. James stopped and stared at the closed door to his bedroom. His chest felt constricted and he was out of breath. It was as if he had aged fifty years since the previous day. James turned the handle, pushed the door open, and dragged his weary body across the floor.

He froze. His chest tightened, and his heart raced as he gazed at the scene in front of him. There she was, lying peacefully on her side. Valentine's loose golden curls had fallen forward and partially covered her face. She had returned home. His Valentine was back.

He wanted to dash across the room, slip into bed, and spend the next several weeks holding her close to him. But he didn't want to risk waking her.

Does she want to stay and give our relationship one more try?

As much as his heart wanted to believe she was back for good, the cynic in him felt it was over. As James juggled his conflicting feelings, he inched towards her. He couldn't stay away.

James sat on the side of the bed. He swept Valentine's blonde locks off her face and behind her ear, then kissed the side of her forehead.

She stirred.

Valentine's eyes flickered, revealing a hint of green, then closed again. James lifted his weary body off the bed and jolted towards the door as Valentine opened her eyes and lifted her head off the duck-egg blue pillowcase.

'I'm sorry.' James's eyes watered. 'I saw you lying there, and I couldn't resist. I'm just—' His voice choked. 'Honestly, I'm just relieved that you're finally safe.'

Valentine pulled back the covers and got out of bed. 'Sorry, I had nowhere else to go. I couldn't go back to that hotel. I hope it's okay that I came back.'

She strolled towards James and wrapped her arms around his waist, then buried her head under his chin. James wrapped his arms around her. His heart raced as he breathed in her scent.

She smelt of freshly cut roses.

He kissed the top of Valentine's head as he drew her closer to his body. She looked up at him. A glaze formed over the top of her eyes as she wept. He took a deep breath. He couldn't stand the sight of her crying and would do anything to make the tears stop. James ran his hands up her body and rested his hand along her jawline. He caressed her rosy-pink lips.

James stepped forward and navigated her across the wooden floor, back to the bed. As James inched closer to the bed, he held Valentine tighter. He kissed her harder, deeper, and with a more fervent, urgent need than he had ever known before. James would never get enough of her.

His blue surgical V-neck shirt floated to the floor, followed by a pair of matching trousers. The lovers inched towards the bed. As he released her lips, Valentine looked into James's eyes, begging him for one more kiss. His warm, trembling hands drifted down her petite frame and, as they reached the bed, paused at her hips. He couldn't resist her gaze any longer. James brushed her lips lightly with his before diving in once more, harder and more intense.

His long fingers glided down to the hem of Valentine's night dress and drew it up towards her hips. James's fingers drifted along her bare skin. His heart raced. He held his breath as he continued to brush his fingers along her porcelain skin.

He pulled away from her soft pink lips. His eyes surveyed the petite woman in front of him. A few moments later, his eyes darted up and met hers. Valentine stared into his eyes as he tore off her blush-pink silk nightdress. He ran his hands down her body and grabbed her thighs, then pulled them up and around his hips. Entwined, they fell into the duck-down duvet. He pressed his lips against hers and groaned.

———

A COLD FOOT brushed against his warm, bare skin and transported James out of his dream state and back to reality. He looked at Valentine snuggled up beside him. She lay there with her eyes open, staring straight ahead, not saying a word.

It wasn't a dream.

James gazed at the ceiling, contemplating whether to break the silence.

Valentine had changed her mind. It was almost too good to be true. James wanted to tell her he had changed and longed to prove it to her. The more cynical part of him thought better of it.

Don't push your luck.

The moment didn't last long, and James couldn't help himself. It slipped out of him like a leaking bucket and poured out onto the floor. All he had to do was stare at the ceiling.

'I'm resigning as the editor.' James rolled over onto his

side, drew Valentine close to him, and entwined himself around her.

'James, I—'

'Just hear me out. I'm going to pursue investigative journalism. It's what I wanted to do after I finished my degree in English literature. And maybe after a few years, after I've created enough contacts, I can leave and freelance.' James looked down as Valentine pulled away from him.

He watched her eyes water.

That's not good.

James pulled her towards him.

'I get that I've been the world's shittiest boyfriend, and I understand why you wanted to leave, but I've realised where I've gone wrong. You and I are important to me.' He kissed her forehead as the tears streamed down, more intense than before.

As she pulled away from James and inched towards the edge of the bed, he grabbed her hand. 'Give me one more chance to make things right.'

Valentine looked away.

'Come back to bed,' James said in a hushed tone.

Valentine pulled away from James's grip. She picked her nightdress off the floor, slipped it over her shoulders, and pulled it down around her slender frame. 'You're never going to change. We both know that. You've always been this guy; I just didn't notice the signs when we first met. I'm going back to Paris,' she said through a sea of tears.

'I can change. Maybe I could come back with you, and we could start again.' James's voice trembled.

'We both know it's over.' Valentine stared at the closed door of the bedroom.

'We could take a break,' James said as a lump formed in the back of his throat.

He knew his pleading would go unheard. Valentine was strong-willed and stubborn. It was these qualities he loved most about her. James couldn't remember when he'd last seen her like this, stubborn and determined. Over the last six months, all she had done was scream at him about the same thing. He would listen and drag his weary body to bed, then wake up and go back to work. It was as if they were passengers on a train who saw each other every day. Strangers who nodded, acknowledging each other's existence.

Merde. She was right.

'I shouldn't have come back here.' Valentine walked towards the door.

'I'm glad you did,' James said as he bit down on his bottom lip. He watched her leave the room.

It was over.

———

HIS REDDENED EYES stared at the letter on the screen. James ran his fingers through his hair. He tilted his head to the side and, with a vacant expression, continued to stare. His entire world had come crashing down in a single moment. But there was one thread left, and he was about to unravel it and wait for it to fall to the floor. Was he making the right decision?

What am I doing? I can't resign.

James got up off his chair and paced the length of the kitchen table. A sharp pain shot up his left thigh, a reminder of the events that had unfolded earlier that morning. Not that he was going to forget any time soon. He hunched over, grabbed the thigh of his blue-and-green-check pyjama trousers, and groaned.

Now that Valentine had left, did any of this even matter? Was he doing this all for her, or was this for him?

He released the grip on his thigh and leaned over the table, resting his left hand on the tabletop, propping himself up.

James turned the computer screen around to face him. His eyes scanned the resignation letter on the screen.

I can't stay here.

James expelled an audible breath. The right path had finally become clear. But could he actually do it? Did he have the tenacity to write an email, attach the letter, and take a leap into the unknown?

As he continued to weigh up the pros and cons, an idea came to mind. It was the perfect distraction. The very thing he needed. Pulling out his smartphone, James typed the following message to his friend Liam. It read: *We should get the guys together and have a reunion dinner. Maybe this summer?*

EPILOGUE

SIX MONTHS LATER

THE QUACKING of a duck jolted James out of his slumber. He looked over at the ringing smartphone on his bedside table and groaned. It was four o'clock in the morning, and the streets of the Upper East Side were bare. New York was still asleep. James leaned over and checked the caller ID. His heart raced as he grabbed the phone and shot out of bed.

Please be good news.

'His lawyer pushed for a quick trial,' the familiar voice of PC Chan said through the speaker, a hint of panic lingering in the air from the early-morning call. 'It was over in a matter of days.'

'The verdict?'

James listened to the PC exhale, and a knot started to form in the pit of his stomach.

'Guilty. At one stage, we didn't think it would end like that.'

James exhaled. His faith in the British justice system was not misplaced.

James's tall, tired frame dropped onto the bed. He pulled at the leg of his pyjama pants as he sat down. James had worked hard to collect evidence to prove Alistair murdered

Pippa and had figured out where he was holding Valentine and Elizabeth. It was a satisfying payoff.

'What did you mean when you said that you didn't think Alistair would get a guilty verdict?' James said with a cold voice.

'Alistair's lawyer was QC Bradley Evans.'

'As in the criminal barrister.' James rolled his eyes and placed his hand on his hip. 'Don't tell me.'

'The judge was Lord William Cavendish. Rumours are going around that they're in the same polo club.'

James froze as the name left Chan's lips. He dismissed the thought. No way.

'Of course, they are.' James placed the smartphone on the bedside table and hit the speaker button.

'He tried to make us look like fools as well,' PC Chan said in a hushed tone. 'Anwar and I didn't have enough time to help the Crown Prosecutor build a case. And the prosecution was understaffed and overworked. But we got lucky.'

'What about the computer found in Pippa's apartment that wasn't present during your initial sweep? Was that included as evidence? Looking back, I now realise that it was probably planted.'

'Yes,' Chan said with a weary tone. 'Alistair did plant evidence that pointed towards Maximilian being a potential suspect. We found his fingerprints on the inside and outside of the puzzle box and on all the jewellery. And we even found his prints on the key to the drawer where you found the puzzle box. So that's why he had to ransack Maximilian's office.'

James sat on the edge of his bed in silence.

'James—' Chan called out from the tiny speaker.

'What about the anonymous major investor behind the dig? Did you meet him? Was he involved?' James bit his lip as he glanced over at his phone.

Chan cleared his throat. 'No, he was only ever present on paper. There were random calls to a US prepaid mobile, but the numbers were dialled once. So, he was smart. But they all said the same thing. It was an anonymous cheque that came in when they needed it.'

'What did Lord William Cavendish say?'

'He didn't push the matter any further.'

James sighed. *Don't ask about her, you fool.*

'I guess you're wondering about Valentine and Elizabeth?'

James leapt off the bed and paced the floor of his bedroom.

'She seemed quite traumatised and is living off the grid.' Chan paused. 'Getting a hold of her was not easy. And Elizabeth is in rehab, thanks to a wealthy benefactor, and Alistair's parents have asked her to be the official resident at the Carmichael Estate.'

Merde. I have to tell him.

Chan sighed. 'You're not going to like this.'

'Just cut to the chase.' James adjusted his posture and turned his ear towards the phone.

'Elizabeth also said you were an editor with empty space on the front page and wanted to create drama to improve the *Northampton Tribune's* falling circulation.'

Why am I not surprised?

'There is nothing wrong with the *Tribune's* circulation. They have a thriving online edition and a wide circulation. That's bullshit.'

A few moments later, James paused in the centre of the room, sprinted over to the bedside table, picked up the phone, and sat.

'What about Maximilian? He knew about Valentine. Remember my recording?'

Chan sighed. 'Upon questioning Maximilian, he revealed that he found out about Valentine sometime on Wednesday morning. He planned to return to the NMA when Alistair was busy on Wednesday evening to release the women and hand them over to the police. And, apparently, he wasn't completely sure if it was Alistair or another interested party. He became suspicious when Alistair texted him about finding a piece of the sword later, on Wednesday evening.'

'And you believe him?'

'Yes, he was very cooperative with the police, to a certain extent.'

'What about the security guards?'

'Retired early.'

'Really?'

'We couldn't get hold of them.'

Chan cleared his throat. 'Anyway, he was caught on a technicality despite their attempts to derail the prosecution. The fingerprint on the ransom note you received matched Alistair. And he slipped up. He knew too much about Pippa's death. In questioning, he let it slip that she was stabbed in the back. He made the stabbing action. Dr Olivier Deschamps said that the stabbing action Alistair made during the interview was the right angle.'

Exhausted, James pulled his weary body off the bed and paced the room for a second time. 'There's something I need to tell you.'

The line fell silent.

'Three months ago, in August, I was involved in a similar case that included a mediaeval artefact. There's a lot I can't talk about because it's a part of an official case that now involves MI6, but I can put you in touch with someone who knows.'

'Who?'

'Her name is Detective Inspector Alice O'Donnell. She works at St Aldgate's Police station in Oxford.' James sighed. 'Chan, this mysterious investor is dangerous. Please be careful, and I mean super careful.'

'That's why you've been changing your number all the time,' Chan said in a high-pitched tone.

'Yeah,' James groaned. 'How are things with you?'

'Fascinating change of topic.'

'Sorry I asked.'

'Well," the other man paused, "you can call me Sergeant Chan from now on, for starters.'

James smiled. 'Since, when?'

'Yesterday, I received the results of my sergeant's exam in the mail. The Super recommended me for the exam after Alistair's arrest. I guess I managed to impress the right people.'

James nodded. 'It was well deserved.'

'Thanks.'

A PAIR of bright blue eyes watched QC Bradley Evans climb into his chauffeur-driven car and head down the Carmichael estate's driveway. Maximilian felt like he was about to make another deal with the devil, a feeling all too familiar to him. But he had no time for guilt. He had responsibilities.

After all, that led him into this mess in the first place—the need to impress his father and make him proud. Deep down, he knew it was a fruitless task but still worth pursuing. It was torture. Now he had to get his parents back. Despite Alistair's attempts to keep the sword for himself and protect his legacy, Maximilian had been working behind the scenes. He did what Alexander wanted, no matter what came his way. And he wanted his parents back and the antidote administered. That was the deal.

'We should be smart about this,' Maximilian said over his shoulder. Then he took a sip of his scotch and stared out the window. 'It makes more sense to tour the sword instead of keeping it in your private collection.'

'Well, you know I'm intrigued,' a man with an American accent said from behind him.

Maximilian turned and stared at the blond curly-haired man, then at his octogenarian assistant, Miles Waterhouse, who was sitting next to him on the sofa. Out of the corner of his eye, Maximilian could see Elizabeth sitting in an armchair, with a smile on her face, without a care in the world. She was quite the actress. Yet, underneath this calm façade of hers was a cyclone of panic and paranoia. Why shouldn't Elizabeth be happy? Alistair's parents loved her like she was their own daughter—they had taken her under their wing. And the Carmichaels had retired to their holiday home in Cannes. She was now the official caretaker of the Carmichael Estate. On top of this, Alexander, the dig's major investor, had paid for her stay in an exclusive rehabilitation centre.

'We could pitch the exhibit to a few museums. New York, Paris, London, Sydney. All of the usual places. Charge an admission fee. We could split the profits between all of the investors,' Maximilian suggested. 'The longer we tour, talk about the sword and its excavation, and point tourists towards Tintagel, the better it will be for everyone. Tintagel will get a much-needed boost in tourism as we promised. And after the tour, the sword could remain in your private collection for further research.'

'What about merchandise?' Alexander brushed the trousers of his charcoal suit, then looked at Maximilian.

'That's a great idea.' Elizabeth got up from her chair and headed to the drinks cart. She paused for a moment. After taking a deep breath, she picked up the bottle of scotch, walked over to Alexander, and poured him a fresh glass.

'So, how are my parents? I trust they are well.' Maximilian placed his scotch glass on the window and walked to the centre of the room, where he sat down in the chair opposite Miles.

'Your father is well.' Alexander sipped his scotch.

'And my mother?'

'I'm sorry to inform you, but the virus has mutated and isn't responding to the medication like the other participants in the previous trials,' Alexander said in a hushed tone. 'She's in my facility in Boston. I'm working on a new formula, but it doesn't look good. I'm afraid she might die before we get a chance to test it.'

'I want my parents back. That was the deal.' Maximilian shot out of the chair and grabbed Alexander by the collar.

Miles stood up and pulled a gun out of his jacket.

'Go on. Shoot me. And after you do, good luck finding the sword. I'm the only one who knows where it's hiding.' Maximilian stared at the old man with his cold, hard, blue eyes. 'I guess you could shoot me, then visit Alistair in jail and ask him—And I don't have to remind you that the police are still looking for you. So good luck with that.'

Alexander waved his hand towards Miles, who put his gun back in his pocket and sat down. 'Threatening and killing me isn't going to bring your mother back.'

'True, but it'll be a nice substitution.' Maximilian released his grip on Alexander's collar. 'No one will miss you once they realise who you really are.' Maximilian towered over Alexander.

'I'm working around the clock to find a cure. It's in my best interests. Imagine the pharmaceutical benefits.'

Maximilian stepped back. 'I want them back.'

'Your father has been released, but he won't leave your mother's side. He's currently staying at the facility, but he can come and go as he pleases,' Alexander said calmly. 'I realise that your family is important. That's natural, so I'll forgive your aggressive outburst.'

'How very magnanimous of you.' Maximilian watched Alexander and Miles get up from the couch.

'You can expect a call from your father in five hours.' Alexander checked his watch.

'I'm returning to Boston to check up on my parents.' Maximilian squinted at the entrepreneur.

'Very well. You can expect your father to meet you at the airport.' Alexander turned around and walked towards the foyer with Miles following closely.

'For a moment, I thought I was going to spend the morning burying two bodies,' Elizabeth mused, standing behind Maximilian.

'Don't put your shovel away too soon.' Maximilian walked to the window and watched the two men climb into the black hire car.

'So, you know where the sword is?' Elizabeth asked as Maximilian turned around. 'All of the pieces?'

Fascinating. She genuinely doesn't know where Alistair hid the sword. I wonder why he never told her about the secret passage in the basement of the NMA. And I wonder what else he's hidden in there?

Maximilian sighed. 'There's one piece with James. And he's now in New York working for the Daily Voice. So I need to get it back, but it's not going to be easy.'

Elizabeth raised her eyebrows.

'I know what you think of me, but I don't like doing these things. I have to.' Maximilian glared at her. 'What other choice do I have?'

ALSO BY A. D. HAY

James Lalonde Amateur Sleuth Mysteries

James Lalonde thought his days of stumbling into murder cases ended with his rookie reporter years. Five years later, as a seasoned editor, he's wrong. From stolen legendary swords to missing manuscripts, James discovers that trouble follows him everywhere, and someone has to solve these crimes.

The Locked Room (Prequel)

It's the opening of Clovervale Hall, an exquisite bed-and-breakfast in England. James Lalonde has an all-expenses-paid trip. But there's one thing he didn't count on—a killer roaming the halls. Soon, James discovers everyone has secrets worth killing for. Can he uncover the truth before the killer strikes again?

The Last Exhibit (Prequel)

When Will Thatcher doesn't show up for work, James Lalonde must attend afternoon tea at the Carmichael Estate. The pleasant gathering ends abruptly when a body is discovered on the front lawn with strange markings on its neck, and a priceless Van Gogh is missing from the wall.

Suspicion (Book 1)

When James Lalonde's girlfriend leaves him, he's forced to cover her story about the local museum's latest acquisition—the legendary sword Excalibur. But when he arrives, Excalibur is missing and there's a dead body at the crime scene. Can James clear his name and find the real killer?

Duplicity (Book 2)

James Lalonde's university reunion takes a deadly turn when a hooded figure murders a professor and steals a priceless mediaeval manuscript, moments after James discovers a secret code within its pages. With his passport confiscated and everyone hiding secrets, can James find the killer before they strike again?

———

Rookie Reporter Series

Five years before James Lalonde discovered that the legendary sword, Excalibur, was stolen from Elizabeth's flat, he was a gofer dreaming of writing his first byline. The Rookie Reporter mystery series follows James's first year as a journalist, starting with his first-ever case.

The Reporter at the Gate (Book 1)

Rookie reporter James Lalonde finally gets his first story - a simple interview with soon-to-be magistrate Albert Harrington. But when he arrives, he finds blood, an empty safe, and no body. With Detective Khan suspecting him of murder, James must clear his name and solve the case before losing his story.

The Woman in the Lake
(Book 2) - Coming Soon

James Lalonde thought being a groomsman at his ex-girlfriend's wedding would be the most awkward part of his weekend. He was wrong. After the bride's body is found floating in the château's lake, he becomes the prime suspect, and awkward becomes deadly. Can James clear his name before the killer strikes again?

AUTHOR'S NOTE

Sometimes, the real and imaginary blend together in fiction. And, Suspicion is no exception. Suspicion is set in Northampton, and I've purposefully avoided using real places with some exceptions. The decision behind this was fuelled by the content of the story. So, if you're a local, you'll notice how many liberties I've taken to create this fictional but a very real city of Northampton.

Real or Not

In particular, on the cover, you'll notice the Northampton Guild Hall. Its facade inspired the Northampton Museum of Anthropology. The surrounding streets and narrow laneways also appear in Suspicion. Yes, I'm sorry to say that this museum is not a real place you can visit.

Fear not you fellow museum buff, there is a museum situated within Cambridge University called the Museum of Archaeology and Anthropology. It's interior, and some of the contents were the inspiration behind the Northampton Museum of Anthropology. I loved this small and very fascinating museum, so much that I used it as a backdrop to the fight scene in chapters thirty-two through to thirty-eight. And, I have to admit it was a super fun and somewhat tragic scene to write because a few of the beautiful artefacts become damaged or broken.

While we're talking about things that aren't quite real, the Northampton Tribune is not a real newspaper, unless there's a small newspaper with a similar name that did not come up during the various stages of research as I wrote and revised Suspicion.

The Chateaux

Yes, the chateaux featured in this book are real. And you can visit both of them. Tintagel which is essentially castle ruins, is in Cornwall and can be visited at certain times of the year. Quite tragically, I was unable to visit these beautiful ruins while I was writing this book because it was closed due to renovations to one of the pedestrian bridges. As you have probably guessed, I'm a bit of a chateaux enthusiast, much like James's grandfather, Dr Francois Lalonde. One of the reasons why I chose this chateaux and Pierrefonds, is due to their connections to Arthurian legend.

The beautiful Chateau de Pierrefonds, which is literally translated from French to English as the castle of Pierrefonds, is in the small French town of Pierrefonds. It's approximately two hours drive from Paris. Unfortunately, I was not able to visit this chateau as well, but this time it was due to the French Railway Strikes making it challenging to travel and hire vehicles during this time. So, in a way, I'm a little jinxed. Or, so it seems. For those of who are Merlin fan's, you will know this is the filming location for Camelot. Thus, this chateau was chosen for its Arthurian connections.

THANK YOU!

Helen Keller said it best: "Alone we can do so little, together we can do so much." And the same is true of publishing a novel, especially for this author.

A huge thank you goes to Paul Teague for his insights as a BBC radio journalist when I was overthinking everything about my story and struggling to inject a sense of realism into the James Lalonde universe. Another thank you goes to the Writers United Facebook Group members who were kind to a stranger with a question who does more lurking than actively participating.

Thanks to Helen Fazal for an initial edit that helped one confused writer improve her revision and self-editing technique. Thank you to my line editor, Angela and my proofreader, Taylor, for helping me create a better story.

This second and third edition of Suspicion would not have been possible without the help of my beta readers, Brandee and Sarah Mae. Special thanks to my Line Editor, Joseph, my copy editor Tony Held for editing the third edition and Dj Hendrickson for proofreading both new and improved editions.

And, a huge thank you to my Mum for not only reading every word I've written but for all the valuable feedback and for highlighting some rather huge and clearly overlooked mistakes during the publishing phase.

Roland, thank you for reading my drafts and encouraging me to keep writing, especially during those times when I could have given up.

ABOUT THE AUTHOR

A. D. Hay is a passionate bibliophile and can usually be found reading a book, and that book will most likely be a murder mystery. She is the author of the *James Lalonde Amateur Sleuth Mystery* and the *Rookie Reporter Amateur Sleuth Mystery* series.

When not absorbed in a gripping page-turner or writing her James Lalonde series, she is a board game addict, loves to travel around Europe, drink tea and rosé, and eat pizza. She is obsessed with journalism, art history and is a closet religious thriller fan.

Born in Brisbane, Australia, she has spent more than a decade in London, where she lives with her husband.

———

You can sign up for a free mystery, The Last Exhibit, behind-the-scenes updates, and bookish research at:
authoradhay.com/read-free/

amazon.com/author/adhay

bsky.app/profile/writeradhay.bsky.social

bookbub.com/authors/a-d-hay

facebook.com/AuthorADHay

goodreads.com/authoradhay

instagram.com/writeradhay

threads.com/@writeradhay

tiktok.com/@authoradhay

x.com/WriterADHay

youtube.com/@AuthorADHay